A summer gift for readers
of Harlequin American Romance

Novellas from three of your favorite authors

The Preacher's Daughter
MARIN THOMAS

A Baby on the Way
LAURA MARIE ALTOM

A Reunion Romance
ANN ROTH

ABOUT THE AUTHORS

Marin Thomas grew up in Janesville, Wisconsin. Like many small-town kids, all she could think about was how to leave once she graduated from high school. Little did she know that her six-foot-one-inch height would be her ticket out. She accepted a basketball scholarship at the University of Missouri in Columbia. After two years, she transferred to the University of Arizona at Tucson. There she developed an interest in fiction writing and obtained a B.A. in radio-television. Her husband's career has taken them to Arizona, California, New Jersey, Colorado, Texas and Illinois, where she currently calls Chicago her home. Marin can now boast that she's seen what's "out there." Amazingly, she's a living testament to the adage "You can take the girl out of the small town, but you can't take the small town out of the girl." Her heart still lies in small-town life, which she loves to write about in her books. You can visit her at www.marinthomas.com or e-mail her at marin@marinthomas.com.

Bestselling, award-winning author **Laura Marie Altom** knew it was time to try her hand at writing when she found herself replotting the afternoon soaps. When not immersed in her next story, Laura enjoys an almost glamorous lifestyle of zipping around in a convertible while trying to keep her dog from leaping out, and constantly striving to reach the bottom of the laundry basket. For real fun, Laura's content to read, do needlepoint and cuddle with her kids and handsome hubby. You can contact her at P.O. Box 2074, Tulsa, OK 74101, or e-mail her at BaliPalm@aol.com. Or you can visit her at www.lauramariealtom.com.

Ann Roth has always been a voracious reader of everything from classics to mysteries to romance. Of all the books she's read, love stories affected her the most and stayed with her the longest. A firm believer in the power of love, Ann enjoys creating emotional stories that illustrate how love can triumph over seemingly insurmountable odds. Ann lives in the greater Seattle area with her husband and a really irritating cat who expects her breakfast no later than 6:00 a.m., seven days a week. You can write Ann by snail mail at Ann Roth, P.O. Box 25003, Seattle, WA 98165-1903, or e-mail her at ann@annroth.net. Or visit her Web site at www.annroth.net to enter the draw for a free book.

Summer Lovin'

Marin Thomas
Laura Marie Altom
Ann Roth

HARLEQUIN®

TORONTO • NEW YORK • LONDON
AMSTERDAM • PARIS • SYDNEY • HAMBURG
STOCKHOLM • ATHENS • TOKYO • MILAN • MADRID
PRAGUE • WARSAW • BUDAPEST • AUCKLAND

ISBN-13: 978-0-373-75169-3
ISBN-10:   0-373-75169-9

SUMMER LOVIN'

Copyright © 2007 by Harlequin Books S.A.

The publisher acknowledges the copyright holders of the
individual works as follows:

THE PREACHER'S DAUGHTER
Copyright © 2007 by Brenda Smith-Beagley

A BABY ON THE WAY
Copyright © 2007 by Laura Marie Altom.

A REUNION ROMANCE
Copyright © 2007 by Ann Schuessler.

This edition published by arrangement with Harlequin Books S.A.

® and TM are trademarks of the publisher. Trademarks indicated with
® are registered in the United States Patent and Trademark Office, the
Canadian Trade Marks Office and in other countries.

www.eHarlequin.com

Printed in U.S.A.

CONTENTS

THE PREACHER'S DAUGHTER

Marin Thomas

Dear Reader,

Remember your first crush? I do. After graduating from college, I ran into the guy I'd worshipped from afar in high school, and my first thought was—yuck, I'm glad I moved on!

But such is not the case for the hero and heroine in my story. For Jake and Amanda, the feelings they had for each other in high school haven't weakened over time. In fact, they've strengthened, keeping them from moving on with their lives and finding someone new to love.

Now fate—or rather, a class reunion—brings them back together after a twenty-year separation. I hope you enjoy watching Jake and Amanda sort out their rocky past as they discover that time and distance have turned their high school crush into real love.

Happy reading!

Marin

For My Sister Amy

Not all daughters are blessed with a mother who loves them as unconditionally as our mother loved us. We must honor her memory by loving our own children the same way. Trust in Mom's love to guide you through the rest of your life. Be brave. Be strong. Be confident. And you will make Mom proud.

Chapter One

Silver Cliff, Colorado. Population 2,307.

The one place Jake Turner had promised himself he'd never return to after his high-school graduation. Yet here he stood in the middle of a Fourth of July barbecue in the city park. Not quite in the middle. More like off to the side—far side. Safely hidden in the shadows of a grouping of birch trees.

The town had changed in the twenty years since he'd sped off on his secondhand motorcycle, but the people hadn't—the pointed stares and burning glances evidence that a two-decade absence had done nothing to alter his bad-boy reputation.

His gut twisted with the urge to run. He wouldn't. Not this time.

A multiyear class reunion, the news that his former alma mater, Silver Cliff High School, was closing its doors and an opportunity to shove his good fortune in his fellow classmates' faces had lured him back for a final goodbye to his childhood home. Jake, voted Least Likely to Succeed, had succeeded. Bigtime.

In truth, his adolescent desire to thrust his accomplishments up the snouts of those who'd scorned him and his mother embarrassed him. But the once-tortured teenager yearned to brag that the town lush's son had become a self-made multimillionaire.

Those reasons aside, Jake was man enough to admit the main motive for his decision to attend the class reunion was Amanda Winslow—the preacher's daughter. The one person who'd actually cared whether Jake earned his high-school diploma.

The only female who'd crossed his mind daily for twenty long years.

For the past half hour he'd searched for Amanda in the swarm of people milling about the park grounds conversing, eating barbecued pork and getting wasted on beer and wine coolers. Over a thousand people were expected to descend upon the small mountain community for the upcoming weekend festivities, and it appeared as if half those people had shown up for the Fourth of July picnic.

Years ago a celebration of this size would have been impossible. Now the increase in B&Bs and motels popping up along the outskirts of town and the recent sale of the high school to a developer who planned to convert the building into high-end condos were evidence that the once-sleepy hollow catered to an exploding tourist population.

Jake didn't give a damn that the town was growing. And he couldn't care less what happened to the high school. If it were up to him, he'd slam a wrecking ball into the eighty-year-old building, which housed nothing but bad memories—except one. *Amanda.*

"Say, is that you, Jake Turner?"

Jake's muscles tensed. "Who wants to know?" He glanced over his shoulder. Thad Trevechy. Aka Einstein. Five feet seven inches of pure scientific brilliance. The teen whiz kid had been the star student in Jake's chemistry class. "Trevechy."

"Hey, you remember me." Einstein stepped forward and shook Jake's hand.

"Haven't changed much," Jake commented, struggling not to stare at the two front teeth protruding from the man's mouth.

"Yep." Trevechy grinned. "Still short and still got buck teeth." He rolled his upper lip back and sniffed like a rabbit. The man had a hell of a sense of humor and could laugh at himself—a trait Jake had yet to acquire.

Trevechy lifted a foot off the ground. "These help."

Circa 1978 platform athletic shoes. "Where'd you find those?"

"Secondhand store in Denver. I got a dress pair for the dinner Saturday. The wife towers over me." Trevechy pointed to a woman checking IDs at the beer tent. "That's Valerie. I rescued her from a life of sin thirteen years ago."

No way could Jake allow that comment to slip by. "What kind of sin?"

"Prostitution."

"You don't say." Jake schooled his features.

"Val used to work Colfax Avenue in downtown Denver."

An image of Einstein trolling the seedy street, searching for a woman to relieve him of his virginity, flashed before Jake's eyes.

"I belonged to a Bible-study group in college and we were sharing the word of the Lord when Val asked me for a prayer sheet."

Trevechy gazed at his wife like a lovesick puppy. "After we prayed together and she agreed to accept the Lord as her savior, I proposed. Then I brought her back to Silver Cliff and Preacher Winslow forgave Val for her seven sins."

"Seven sins?"

"She'd just begun her career when we met. There wasn't a whole lot of sinning to forgive. Afterward, the preacher baptized her and married us."

Jake would have loved to be present when Trevechy had shown up on the preacher's doorstep with a hooker on his arm. Jake had had his share of run-ins with Amanda's father. Over the years he'd been the recipient of sermons and stern warnings. In one ear and out the other—until he'd returned home one night the summer before his senior year and found Amanda's father in bed with his mother.

Jake's mother had been no innocent. She'd been a drunk and, yes, sometimes a whore. But the one person in their community who should have offered sympathy, protection and forgiveness abused her in an inexcusable way.

Little did Amanda realize that she'd offered Jake the perfect opportunity for revenge when she'd insisted on tutoring him their senior year. He'd had one goal in mind—lure the preacher's daughter into his bed and ruin her. He hadn't counted on falling head over heels for Amanda. They'd almost had sex once, but a guilty conscience had stopped Jake. He hadn't been able to hurt Amanda in such a cruel way.

Several times he'd been tempted to expose Amanda's father—but what purpose would it have served, other than destroying her family? He'd had to leave town after graduation. Had he stuck around, he had no doubt Amanda would have landed in his bed and ended up hating him. "Glad things worked out for you, Trevechy." At least someone was happy with their life turned out.

"Val opened a new business a few years ago. The Loving Hands Daycare."

Swallowing a groan, Jake choked, "What do you do for a living?"

"I'm an engineering professor at the University of Colorado in Boulder. I teach correspondence courses through the cable TV network and the Internet."

"Sounds interesting."

"The hours are great. Plenty of free time to help Val with our kids." Trevechy stuffed his hands into the front pockets of his plaid golfing shorts. "What's your story? You skipped town right after graduation."

"Went to California and hired on with a software company." Jake rolled his shoulders under the weight of the lie. He didn't work for the company—he owned it. "The class reunion gave me an excuse to tie up a few loose ends."

Trevechy chortled. "One of those loose ends is still around, if you're interested."

Memories lived on forever in small-town minds. Jake supposed everyone assumed he'd had a crush on the petite, soft-spoken blonde after their public kiss following their high-school graduation ceremony.

"Amanda was scheduled to help with the reunion registration early this morning. Did you stop by the Silver Palace?"

"Not yet." Whether Jake remained for the weekend of festivities depended on Amanda.

"My wife and Amanda are good friends. Valerie walks the day-care kids to the library once a week for story time." When Jake didn't comment, Trevechy carried the conversation by himself. "Amanda also tutors."

The tutoring comment triggered memories of Amanda… *"C'mon, Jake. Stop goofing off and solve the math equation."*

When Amanda had learned that their class might be the first in the history of the school to fail to graduate all its students— meaning Jake—she'd decided to tutor him. After the way her father had used his mother, Jake had wanted nothing to do with the preacher's daughter. When he'd rebuffed her offer, she'd nagged him in detention every day.

"I don't need your help, Ms. Brain."

"Yes, you do." She'd leveled a glare at him.

"Go find another charity case."

"Sorry. I handle one charity case at a time." Amanda had been so sweetly determined that Jake had been left momentarily speechless.

"What if I refuse?"

"Then I'll sit here until you change your mind."

Amanda's resolve offered him the perfect opportunity to seek revenge against her father, but he had to be sure she was in for the long haul. *"People will talk."*

"Gossip doesn't bother me." That she didn't appear concerned his mother was a drunk and the only person in town receiving public assistance baffled him.

"Please, Jake. Just try. For me."

He couldn't say for certain whether it was his need for vengeance or her sincerity, but he hadn't been able to resist her plea.

Each F Jake earned caused Amanda to dig in her heels and push harder. Her gutsy I'm-not-quitting-on-you attitude had won his admiration, further screwing with his evil intent to destroy her father. By the second quarter of the year, he'd quit skipping school and had handed in all his homework on time. Their combined efforts had paid off—Jake had graduated.

Dragging his mind away from memory lane, he murmured, "Amanda must be good at what she does if she's been head librarian the past five years." He could easily picture the blonde sharing her love for learning and reading with children.

"How'd you know she was head librarian?"

Refusing to confess he'd spied on Amanda over the years, Jake lied, "Can't remember where I heard it."

When Jake had ridden away from Silver Cliff, he'd intended to forget the place and everyone in it. But his attempts to purge Amanda from his thoughts and heart had failed. Four years after leaving town he'd subscribed to Silver Cliff's weekly *Jotter*—aka gossip tabloid.

Through the paper he'd learned that Amanda had graduated from Colorado State University and been hired as an assistant librarian for Silver Cliff's library located in the basement of town hall. Five years ago, an announcement appeared in the *Jotter* that she'd been promoted to head librarian.

The one piece of news he'd expected—dreaded reading—

had never materialized. As far as he knew, Amanda had never been engaged or married. Jake planned to learn if what he'd felt for her all those years ago had been a simple high-school crush or something deeper. He suspected the *something deeper* was the cause of his tightly wound body.

"Weatherman says we might hit eighty this afternoon."

C'mon, Amanda. Rescue me from Einstein.

"Well, aren't you a sight for sore eyes—Jake Turner, as I live and breathe."

The sound of the familiar voice sent Jake's heart into an uncontrolled spin. He shifted, his gaze colliding with the woman who'd haunted his memory for twenty long years. *She's breathtaking.* For a fraction of a second, time stopped and he and Amanda were back in high school.

If possible, she was more beautiful than he'd remembered. Twenty years had lent her heart-shaped face an appealing air of maturity and confidence. The wind caught her honey-blond hair and his hands trembled with the memory of sliding his fingers through the silky strands. Her incredible blue eyes, wiser with age, pulled him in as they had when they were teenagers. If not for the faint lines fanning from their outer corners, she could pass for a college coed.

Tongue-tied, he stumbled over the words, "You haven't changed a bit, Amanda. You're prettier than ever."

Pink tinged her cheeks. "You've grown an inch or two since high school." She edged closer, bringing into light the differences in their height. At six-three, Jake towered over Amanda's five-foot-six-inch frame, making him feel the urge to protect and shelter her. A ridiculous notion, considering how the woman possessed more resolve than anyone he'd ever met.

"Hello, Thad," she greeted Einstein, who stood to the side, an amused expression on his face.

Trevechy cleared his throat. "Time to check in with the

boss." Waving, he walked off toward the beer tent, leaving Jake alone with Amanda and a bad case of the nerves.

"There's something different about you, but I can't—"

"The glasses," she interrupted, fluttering her light brown lashes. "I wear contacts now."

Was she flirting with him? Pulse thundering, he teased, "I was fond of those owl-rimmed spectacles."

Sultry laughter grabbed Jake by the gut and yanked. There was no doubt in his mind that his feelings for Amanda all those years ago remained alive and strong. "Don't worry. You still look intellectual, Ms. Brain," he added with a grin.

AMANDA LAUGHED good-naturedly. Twenty years had mellowed her reaction to her high-school nickname—*Brain.* Heavens, how she'd hated that moniker. So what if her IQ bordered on genius? Jake Turner had always held a special place in her heart because he'd been the first guy to see her as a flesh-and-blood human and not a robot or computer. And he'd been her first *crush.* A crush she suddenly was certain she'd never gotten over.

Amanda couldn't take her eyes off Jake. Silver Cliff's bad boy had changed. His once-wiry build had transformed into solid muscle and broad shoulders. The goatee was new. The short black beard lent him an air of danger. Not that he needed an *air* to make him stand out in a crowd. Her gaze zeroed in on his mouth, and his lips spread into a smile. The past tumbled forward as she recalled their high-school graduation ceremony. After he'd received his diploma and walked off the auditorium stage, he'd planted an open-mouth-lots-of-tongue kiss on her in front of God and everyone. Then, like a Hollywood movie, he'd hopped on his motorcycle and sped out of town, leaving Amanda with a broken heart.

Lips tingling anew from the memory, she forced her attention from his face to his coal-black hair. He wore his hair a tad shorter than in high school, the shaggy style barely brushing the tops of his shoulders. She recalled the time Principal Mahoney had threatened to chop Jake's hair off if he didn't cut it. The next day Jake had returned to school with a quarter inch of cut hair in a sandwich bag and tossed it on Mahoney's desk. Poor Jake. The principal had had it out for him all four years of high school.

Jake's shaggy mop added to his sex appeal, but his dark brown eyes were what intrigued Amanda most. Years ago, she swore she'd caught a glimpse of his tortured soul. Today, however, the dark orbs remained guarded. The chip on his shoulder was still there—otherwise, why would he have stood off by himself, observing, instead of joining in the festivities? Regardless, she detected a maturity in Jake that hadn't been present in high school. He might not be comfortable around others, but he appeared at ease with himself—as if he'd come to terms with who he'd become.

The new Jake Turner definitely intrigued her. "I guess you received the reunion announcement." She'd sent the invitation to the only address Jake's mother had had for him. Not in a million years had she expected the man to attend the extravaganza.

"I got it." He watched a group of children gathered near a clown creating balloon animals.

"So you decided to attend at the last minute?" She was on the reunion committee and knew for a fact he hadn't RSVP'd.

Jake narrowed his eyes. "The reunion gave me an excuse to clear up some unfinished business in town."

Amanda wondered if his *unfinished* business had something to do with her. In case she didn't have another chance, she offered, "Thank you for the generous cashier's check you sent after your mother's death." Part of the money had been meant to bury his mother, Susan; the other, he'd insisted Amanda use for the library. When he didn't respond, she touched his arm. "I'm sorry about your mother."

Her breath caught at the flash of vulnerability in his eyes. "Thanks." Then he glanced at her bare ring finger.

Ask him. She was thirty-seven—almost thirty-eight. If Jake was attached or even remotely involved with another woman, she'd wish him well and move on to…to…nothing. "Did you bring anyone special with you this weekend?"

"No," he murmured, then added in a husky whisper, "I haven't been involved with a woman for a long time."

Flustered and excited by his admission, she motioned to the food tent. "Hungry?"

"Not particularly." His penetrating stare made her nervous—in a good way. "Feel like going for a ride on my bike?" he asked.

"You still have that beat-up old motorcycle?"

A huge grin wreathed his face, reminding her of the *hot* guy she'd fallen head over heels for twenty years ago. He nodded to a brand-new Harley-Davidson parked along the street.

"Wow." For someone with a high IQ she sure had a limited vocabulary.

"What do you say we take it for a spin."

A ride on a Harley with Silver Cliff's notorious bad boy…what more could a *brain* want?

Chapter Two

Wearing Jake's helmet and black leather jacket, which smelled of musk cologne and pure Jake, Amanda wrapped her arms around his middle and lifted her face to the sun as the Harley sped along the mountain road.

The bike dipped around a sharp curve and she tightened her hold on his trim waist. Exhilaration whipped her body and she was tempted to stick out her hand and skim her fingers along the pavement. Jake's ability to thrill hadn't diminished with the passing of time. He made her long to take risks. Made her feel alive!

Amanda had been waiting for this moment—Jake Turner's return—and she didn't intend to waste a minute of their time together. As long as she didn't fall under his spell again, life would go on as normal after he rode off into the sunset—without her.

Are you kidding? Amanda focused on the rev of the engine, hoping to block out the voice in her head.

You're as stuck on the man today as you were twenty years ago. Maybe even more, seeing how your heart flipped when you spotted him in the park.

Yes, she'd been shocked Jake had shown up for the reunion. He was the last person she'd expected to attend from their graduating class. Still, hanging out with him during the next few days would be a nice diversion from her day-to-day routine.

Routine? Don't you mean boring life?

Her life wasn't that bad. She had friends. A good job. A nice little home.

No husband. No children. No lover. *Some life.*

Jake's return would change nothing. She was under no illusions that being with him would evolve into anything other than a weekend of fun.

So you're afraid to hope for more?

No. Maybe. Yes! She was afraid to wish Jake's feelings for her might be more than simple nostalgia. After all, they'd almost made love the night before their high-school graduation ceremony. But something had stopped Jake.

"What's wrong?" Amanda had begged, her hands grasping Jake's waist, to pull him back on top of her.

"I can't do this." He pushed himself off the bed.

Amanda had assumed Jake was nervous about making love in her bedroom. *"Don't worry. My parents won't be home until midnight."*

"I'm not worried."

She'd yanked the sheet over her bare breasts and sat up. *"Then why won't you make love to me?"* Amanda had never seen Jake so tormented before.

He'd shoved a hand through his mussed hair. *"Because everything's all screwed up."*

"What's screwed up?"

"My feelings for you, damn it."

"Are you saying you don't care about me anymore?"

His hand turned the doorknob. *"I'm saying I care too much."*

"What does that mean?"

"This is so wrong." He shook his head. *"I'm sorry, Amanda."*

That was the last time he'd spoken to her. After the graduation ceremony, he'd kissed her, then left town for good.

Forcing her thoughts away from analyzing her and Jake's past, present and future relationship, she envisioned her strait-laced, rigid father's expression at catching her riding on the back of Jake Turner's Harley and laughed. Jake glanced over his shoulder and flashed a devil-may-care grin.

His smile reminded her of the day she'd walked into the detention room in the basement of the high school and offered her tutoring services. He'd been the only one in the room—par for the course since the rest of the students in their class were passing all their courses. Sitting at a desk in the far corner, he'd glared, daring her to reach out.

The thought of running had crossed her mind until she'd glimpsed the yearning in his eyes. He'd insisted he didn't need her help and that he wasn't a charity case. He'd attempted to frighten her off by arguing that people would talk behind their backs. Then all of a sudden he quit protesting. He opened his math book and muttered, "Knock yourself out." They'd formed a fragile bond that day that had deepened with each tutoring session.

Jake left the highway and drove along a dirt-packed path up into the mountains. Amanda was familiar with the route. The road led to Jake's childhood home—what was left of it, anyway. The home that had caused him pain and heartache, much of which she'd only learned about after befriending his mother a few years before the woman had died.

Through the stories Susan had shared, Amanda had come to understand why Jake couldn't leave town fast enough following graduation. Part of her envied him for having the courage to forge a new life away from Silver Cliff.

Amanda had chosen a different path—that of the dutiful daughter. After graduating from college, she'd returned to live temporarily in Silver Cliff while she searched for a job. She received an offer for a librarian position at a high school in Littleton, but before she'd even had her bags packed, her mother had suffered a series of ministrokes.

With her mother facing months of rehabilitation, Amanda hadn't had the heart to leave her solely in the hands of Amanda's aging father. Over time, it became obvious that Amanda's mother would never fully recover from the effects of the strokes. That on top of developing postmenopausal osteoporosis had left her mother weak and vulnerable. So Amanda had resigned herself to staying in Silver Cliff and watching over her parents.

When her father had announced five years ago that he and Amanda's mother intended to retire to an assisted-living facility in Florida, no one had been more shocked than Amanda. Finally free of the responsibility of her parents, she'd considered moving elsewhere. But the idea of beginning over again alone at the age of thirty-two had held little appeal.

The only one in their sixteen-member graduating class to remain in Silver Cliff, she'd been dreading attending the class reunion without a date. Enter her white knight—Jake Turner. His sudden appearance had Amanda wondering if it was time for her life to change course—maybe in the direction of the man she had her arms wrapped around.

Jake slowed the bike to a stop several feet from the one-story dilapidated shack. The roof had caved in this past winter under the weight of repeated snowfalls. The windows had been broken out and the furniture, not that there had been much, lay in mildewy ruin. Just as well she and Jake couldn't enter. He shouldn't view the spray-painted messages on the walls that vandals had left behind—DRUNKEN WHORE. BITCH. TRAMP.

Amanda slipped off the bike, removed her helmet and set it on the leather seat. Towering evergreens surrounded the house on three sides, creating a natural windbreak. Jake approached the bottom porch step and studied the front door, which hung crookedly on rusted hinges. After a moment he bent his head and rubbed his brow.

Amanda's heart ached at the forlorn picture he made and she yearned for the power to erase his childhood and replace the memories with better ones. He held out a hand, summoning her.

She hurried to his side, sliding her fingers along his palm. His grip was warm and sure—yet a little needy. He nodded toward the flower bed on the east side of the cabin, which received a good portion of sunlight each day. "Someone's been weeding my mother's garden."

He'd noticed. "Me." After graduating from college and returning to Silver Cliff, Amanda had told her parents that she'd planned to visit Susan. She'd been feeling nostalgic and had hungered for news about Jake. Her father had become angry and had asked that she have nothing to do with a woman of loose morals. Hating to see her father so upset, Amanda had acceded to his wishes.

Now that she thought about it, the one and only instance she'd held her ground with her folks had been when they'd demanded she stop tutoring Jake because *a boy like that* would soil her reputation. When her father had been confronted by his parishioners, who'd frowned upon his daughter's involvement with Susan Turner's illegitimate son, her father had been forced to resort to the standard it's-the-Christian-thing-to-do sermon.

After Amanda's parents had moved to Florida, she immediately sought out Susan and made an effort to become better acquainted with her. Jake's mother had invited Amanda to visit at the cabin. In the end, when Susan had been too sick to garden, Amanda had helped her to a chair in the yard, where she could watch Amanda tend to her beautiful flowers.

Susan had shared numerous memories of Jake's childhood

with her. Most of them were sad, but a few had been sweet. The memories had made Amanda feel closer to Jake. After Susan died, she'd continued to tend the garden because she hadn't been willing to give up the only connection she'd had to Jake. "I spent many afternoons with your mother in her garden. We were good friends at the time of her death."

"Friends?" Jake's eyes narrowed as if searching for a hidden meaning behind the word.

Amanda eased her hand from his and strolled to the edge of the flower bed. There, she knelt and commenced pulling weeds. "One afternoon your mother showed up at the library and checked out a book on ovarian cancer. She'd never admitted to being ill, but it wasn't long before her body showed signs of the disease."

Jake's large-booted foot appeared next to Amanda's thigh. "Why didn't she seek medical treatment?"

"Your mother didn't have insurance." Amanda glanced up and winced at the guilty flush suffusing his face.

"If I'd known, I would have sent more money," he whispered.

"She didn't want you to know, Jake." Amanda tugged his pant leg and he squatted next to her on the grass. "Susan confessed that you'd been mailing her a monthly allowance for years. She believed it was more than she deserved."

A nerve along Jake's jaw throbbed and Amanda decided to change the subject. "She had a lot to say about you."

"I'm surprised she could recall anything after drinking herself stupid for years." As much as Jake wished others to believe he hated his mother, Amanda sensed that he hungered for information about her.

"Susan admitted she was a horrible mother to you."

His eyes widened. "She did?"

"Yes. And more." Yearning to offer comfort, but believing he wouldn't accept it, she settled for leaning against his side.

"Susan claimed your father had broken her heart when he'd walked out on the two of you. She mourned the loss of his love so deeply that she gave up on anyone or anything."

"No shit." Jake shot off the ground and turned his back to Amanda, his chest heaving, his lungs struggling for air.

"Before she died she asked me to tell you that you were the one bright spot in her life and she was sorry you'd been stuck with her for a mother."

Sorry. His mother was *sorry?*

The little boy in Jake struggled not to raise his fist to the heavens and shout, *No! No! I won't forgive you!* But the man in him understood the futility in holding a grudge against a dead woman. Why hadn't his mother reached out to him after he'd begun sending money? He might have reached back. Maybe he would have returned home. Maybe she would have begged for his forgiveness. Maybe he would have offered it.

Heck of a lot of maybes…

Amanda stood and clasped his shoulder. He tensed, then relaxed as the warmth of her comforting touch seeped through his T-shirt. "She also wanted you to understand the reason she never celebrated your birthday."

"Let me guess. My mother regretted getting pregnant with me."

"No." Amanda slipped around him and gazed up at his face. For a second he forgot everything and lost himself in her bottomless blue eyes…eyes that saw into his soul, saw his pain, his hunger, the yearning for her that he couldn't hide.

"On your first birthday, your father walked out on you and your mother for good. From that day on, every Fourth of July was a reminder that another year had passed and your father hadn't returned."

Jake ached for his mother. But if she'd loved his father that deeply how could she have allowed herself to be exploited by other men…by Amanda's father? "What do you expect me to say? That I forgive my mother? That I understand?" Shoot, his kindergarten teacher had been the one to inform him that his birthday was the Fourth of July.

"Follow me." Amanda grabbed his hand and strolled to the far end of the garden. "Notice that cluster of blue and white flowers in the corner?" She pointed several yards away.

"What's special about them?" He could get accustomed to the feel of her fingers entwined with his.

"Those are the first perennials your mother planted in honor of your birthday. Every Fourth of July since you graduated from high school and left town, Susan planted a new flower to commemorate your birthday. After she died, I carried on the tradition." Amanda indicated a small mound of freshly churned dirt. "Canterbury bells. I planted them early this morning."

Jake's throat constricted. After a twenty-year separation Amanda still cared. Otherwise why would she have gone to all the trouble of planting a flower for him each year on his birthday? He studied her pretty face almost believing her goodness had the power to erase the past. To make him forgive her father's sin.

"Happy birthday, Jake," she murmured, then did the most amazing thing—rose on tiptoe and kissed him. A gentle, chaste caress.

"That's the nicest birthday gift I've ever received."

Amanda clasped his face between her hands. "Your mother loved you. In her own way. As much as she could."

"I'm glad she had you and wasn't alone at the end. Thank you for making sure she was buried in the church cemetery."

A sheepish expression crossed Amanda's face and she wiggled loose. "Actually, Susan wanted to be buried here." Amanda motioned to a subtle swell of earth beneath a large evergreen. "She said that when you were little, you hid in the tree while she entertained…"

"It was either that or get slapped around by one of her

drunken boyfriends." Jake remembered waking in the middle of one freezing October night to find a warm quilt shoved up under the branches within his reach. Maybe his mother had loved him.

"You'd told your mother the tree made you feel safe. Near her death, she asked to be buried by the tree because she craved to feel that same safeness."

Jake averted his face and battled the stinging sensation biting his eyes. *Damn it*. His mother didn't deserve his tears. But in his mind he heard her voice begging for him to come to her. He stood at the foot of the tree, the mound blurring before his eyes.

What was left to say?

I'm sorry my father broke your heart, Mom. Sorry you couldn't move past the pain to love me the way a mother should love her child. Sorry I never returned home before you died.

He sucked in a deep breath and tilted his face to the sky. Regrets—those would never disappear. But it was time to move on. Time to forgive—his mother, at least. *No more worries, Mom. Rest in peace now.*

Feeling as if a heavy weight had been lifted from his shoulders, he returned to Amanda and brushed a strand of hair from her eyes. He'd settled the past with his mother. But what about Preacher Winslow? What about Amanda? Would she forgive him when she found out the truth behind their past relationship? With deliberate concentration, he shoved the worries aside and focused on the crazy way Amanda made him feel.

"Do you remember the bet I made with you our senior year?"

A tiny line formed between her brows, then her mouth widened into a smile. "Something to do with teaching the preacher's daughter how to drink."

Jake laughed, suddenly very glad he'd garnered the courage

to revisit Silver Cliff. "My turn to be the tutor. By the end of tomorrow night's reunion mixer you'll be the best tequila-shooter drinker west of the Rocky Mountains."

"If I promise to be attentive during the tutoring session, will you take me to the fireworks tonight at Canyon Lake?"

Was she crazy? Of course he'd attend the fireworks with her…and maybe they'd even set off a few of their own.

Chapter Three

Thump. Thump. Thump, thump.

"Amanda Winslow, open up. I know you're in there!"

"Hold on to your hat, Valerie," Amanda grumbled, then almost fell headfirst down the stairs when she stepped on the hem of her long prairie skirt. "Where's the fire?" she demanded after opening the front door.

"Nope, that'll never do." Valerie Trevechy stepped into the house, shut the door, took Amanda by the elbow and tugged her back up the stairs. "If you're going out with Jake Turner, you'd better ditch the schoolmarm image or he'll ride off into the sunset on that sexy Harley all by his lonesome."

Outweighed by at least seventy pounds, Amanda had little choice but to allow her friend to drag her into the bedroom. "Who told you I was going to the fireworks with Jake?" she huffed, then collapsed on the end of the bed.

Valerie sent her a *duh* stare. "Thad said Jake showed up at the picnic this afternoon and chatted with you." She crossed the room to Amanda's closet. "And shame on you for not sharing that tidbit of news with your best friend."

Guilty as charged. Amanda hadn't wanted to confide that Jake had agreed to take her to Canyon Lake tonight. Not when a tiny part of her feared he might stand her up. "I didn't tell anyone," she insisted.

"You didn't have to." Valerie rolled her eyes. The woman ought to live in Hollywood where her acting skills might be more appreciated. "Everyone remembers you had a crush on Jake in high school. He shows up for the reunion—single— and of course people are going to assume you two will be attending the festivities together."

"You didn't go to high school in Silver Cliff. How do you know anything?" Amanda grumbled.

"I listen to gossip. And don't assume folks have forgotten the KISS."

"People are talking about the kiss he gave me at graduation?" Thank God no one found out about the almost-sex episode in her bedroom the night before. With her luck, one of her father's former parishioners would phone her parents in Florida and alert them to Jake's presence in town.

Valerie grinned. "The way I heard, the smooch was more like a wild, erotic exploration of your mouth in front of the whole town."

Flinging her arms out to her sides, Amanda fell backward onto the bed. She'd been secretly thrilled that Jake had decided to attend the reunion, but everyone sticking their noses in her business spoiled some of the fun.

"Where's he staying?" Valerie sank to her knees and rummaged through shoe boxes. "I phoned Julia and she claims he hasn't checked into the Rosemary House or any of the other bed-and-breakfasts in the area. Sandy called the motels on the outskirts of town and he wasn't registered at any of them."

Amanda's stomach sank. Maybe Jake had never intended to stay.

"Unless…" Valerie held up a pair of black boots. "He's staying with you."

"In my house?" Amanda gasped, hoping she'd put the right amount of outrage in her response to prevent her friend from guessing that she'd planned all along to offer Jake her guest bedroom.

"What's wrong with him sleeping here?" Valerie argued. "You've got two bedrooms—not that one isn't plenty." She reached inside the closet and removed a short, above-the-knee black silky skirt. "Slinky, sexy and sure to rev his engine."

"People will see the color of my underwear when we zip through town on his Harley." Hence the prairie skirt and its ten yards of material.

"Poor sport." Valerie exchanged the skirt for a pair of designer jeans.

"My butt looks too big in those," Amanda whined.

"Listen, sweetie, you're talking to a woman who understands a thing or two about butt size—mainly that it expands with childbirth. In my opinion, there ought to be a special place in hell for skinny women who complain that they're fat. Your whole butt isn't half the size of one of my cheeks." She wiggled the hanger. "Besides, a man needs a little teasing now and then to keep him interested. You wear these and his hands will itch to make a grab for your fanny."

Amanda imagined Jake's big hands on her fanny and muttered, "Give 'em here." She shimmied into the pair, then sucked in her stomach in order to zip them.

"Perfect. Now, where's that sexy white blouse with all the ruffles? You wore it for the pirate-book day at the library."

"Too fancy for jeans," Amanda protested.

"C'mon, where is it?" Valerie attacked the dresser, opening and closing the drawers.

Disgusted with herself for not putting up a fight, Amanda retrieved the shirt from the closet, then slipped it on and studied her reflection in the mirror attached to the inside of the closet door. *Hmm. Not bad.*

"Now the boots. Jake's taller than you, so he'll appreciate the two-inch heels when you kiss."

Blushing, Amanda grabbed the boots off the floor, shoved her feet into them and blurted, "No more. If he doesn't like what he sees—"

"He likes what he sees just fine," a deep voice echoed through the room.

Both females spun and gaped at Jake, lounging in the doorway. He shrugged. "I rang the bell."

"The bell's broken." Both females spoke in unison.

"I heard arguing—"

"We were discussing Amanda's wardrobe," Valerie interrupted. "You must be Jake. I'm Thad's wife, Valerie."

Jake shook her hand. "Nice to meet you."

"I was just leaving." She winked at Amanda, then sauntered out of the room.

There ought to be a place in hell—preferably right next to the skinny women—for best friends who think they know it all.

Oh, my, Jake Turner stood in her bedroom. Images from the past—a different bedroom, a younger Jake—blurred before her eyes, landing her momentarily speechless.

"You look great, Amanda." His gaze traveled the length of her body, then settled on the pink satin comforter behind her. "Ready?"

Amanda wondered if *ready* referred to leaving for the fireworks or jumping into bed with her.

IN JAKE'S MIND, Canyon Lake was one of the best-kept secrets in the entire state of Colorado and it was right in Silver Cliff's own backyard. Located a short distance outside of town, the lake was small compared with others in the area. But the beauty of the majestic rocky walls that surrounded three sides of the water hole made the picnic getaway a favorite for locals and tourists.

Jake slowed the Harley to a crawl and called over his shoulder, "The entire town is heading to the lake." They'd been trailing several school buses that had been rented to transport class-reunion attendees to the fireworks. Add residents from neighboring communities and Jake suspected securing a patch of grass to sit on would be impossible.

When he turned at the entrance to the state park, he squeezed the handlebars and fought the tightening sensation in his chest. In high school he'd never attended any of the dances or athletic events. When Amanda had asked why, he'd confessed that he hated crowds. Spending tonight with hundreds of people wasn't his idea of fun. But he was willing to ignore his discomfort to please Amanda.

No sense sitting shoulder to shoulder when there were plenty of out-of-the-way places to watch the fireworks. He pointed a few yards ahead of the bus in front of them. "Hang on. I'm taking the dirt path." Amid several horn blasts, he swerved the bike off the road and onto the trail. They climbed in elevation, until the path dead-ended several hundred feet above the grassy banks of the lake. After parking the bike, he grabbed Amanda's hand and strolled to the edge of the clearing. "Now, this is a view."

"It's beautiful," Amanda agreed.

Jake slid an arm around her waist and pulled her near. A light breeze played with her hair, blowing several strands against his chest. He bent his head and nuzzled her neck. "You smell good."

"Mmm." She tilted her head, exposing more of her neck. He kissed the soft skin beneath her ear. Twenty years hadn't changed his body's reaction to Amanda. She challenged... excited...teased him.

Jake flashed a sexy grin and tilted her chin. He bent his head, pausing for a moment, allowing her a chance to refuse his kiss. She didn't. The first touch of her mouth brought back memories of a sweet, inexperienced girl. The memories lasted only a moment, because Amanda's kiss now wasn't the tentative flirting of lips he remembered. Her tongue thrust boldly into his mouth, sweeping the inside before retreating. He wanted to reciprocate with his tongue, but she broke off the kiss and stepped back.

"I didn't know librarians could kiss like that," he teased.

"I had a good teacher." She motioned to the lake. "The water is beautiful from up here."

The sunset washed across the lake's surface, transforming the water into a dance of sparkling light. One end of the lake appeared blue-black, the other light turquoise. From this elevation he couldn't spot any trout, but the crowd gathering along the banks would be able to view the fish as far as twenty feet out and six feet deep.

"Let's sit down." They returned to the Harley and he removed the quilt from the storage compartment, and together they spread the blanket across the ground and sat.

"I have a confession to make," she admitted.

"You mean this is where you tell me you're involved with someone?" He meant it as a joke, but he held his breath, hoping he hadn't guessed right.

"No." She punched him playfully in the chest. "I remembered you didn't like crowds, so I expected you to stand me up tonight."

"You're right. I'm not a people person."

"Why?" she probed.

"After a while I got tired of the insults. As a kid, I could fight back. But in high school the fistfights didn't go over well with Principal Mahoney. I figured out quickly that I was always the one punished when a fight broke out. Didn't matter who threw the first punch, my butt landed in detention. So I avoided people. Avoided fighting."

Stretching out on her side, she rested her chin in the palm of her hand and Jake had to force his gaze away from the front of her blouse, which stretched taut against her breasts.

"Growing up in a small town was difficult for you, wasn't it?" she stated.

"Yeah, life sucked. I didn't have a dad or a big brother to defend me. And half the time my mom was too drunk to care what other people said about us. But looking back on those years now…things could have been worse."

Amanda entwined her fingers with his and offered, "I'm sorry, Jake."

That Amanda cared about his childhood consoled him. "What about you? Being the preacher's daughter must have been rough."

"You're the only person who's ever acknowledged that maybe my life wasn't as sweet and heavenly as my parents portrayed it to be. Having a brother or sister to share the spotlight would have helped. Instead I alone bore the brunt of my parents' undivided— and most of the time—unwanted attention." Her heavy sigh tugged at Jake's heart. "I was expected to be Miss Perfect—say the right thing, act the right way, reflect well on my father, be an extension of my mother."

"I got the feeling your old man didn't want me anywhere near you." Jake watched Amanda's face for a sign that she understood what her father had done to his mother. But her expression revealed nothing.

"No, he didn't want me to tutor you. Threatened to ground me if I continued. I didn't care."

"So that's the real reason you tutored me—to rebel against your father?"

"At first it was an act of rebellion. But…" Her gaze skittered away. "The more time we spent together, the more I wished to get to learn about the real Jake Turner." She rolled onto her back and stared at the darkening sky. "And I suspected we had more in common than we realized."

"How so?" He whisked a strand of hair from her cheek, his fingers lingering against her skin, making her heart hold its breath.

"We both wanted out of Silver Cliff."

"How come I was the only one who blew off this place?" Jake challenged.

"I tried," she protested with a weak smile. "After I graduated from college, I had a job offer at a high school in Littleton. I accepted the position, but then my mother suffered a series of strokes. My father needed help caring for her, and well—" she fluttered a hand in the air "—I landed a job as assistant librarian at the Silver Cliff Library. I thought my mother would recover and that the move home would be temporary. But temporary turned into sixteen years."

Amanda was a better person than Jake. Her parent had required help and she'd been there. Although Jake's mother had never put out a call for help, he believed deep in his gut that she'd needed him. But he'd stayed away because he'd intended for her to pay for his cruddy childhood. Too bad life didn't come with do-overs. "You did what any dutiful daughter would. Besides, look at you now—head librarian. That's impressive."

"Don't get me wrong. I love my job, but…" She sat up. "Enough about me. What about—"

"Not so fast. I've got one more question," he cut in. "Why haven't you ever married?"

She tucked her legs to the side. "How did you learn I never married?"

"No engagement announcement in the *Jotter.*"

"You have a subscription to the *Silver Cliff Jotter*?"

"Yes, ma'am." He grinned.

"Jake Turner, you've been spying on me all these years?" Amanda wasn't sure if she was flattered or offended that he'd kept track of her since high school.

"Guilty as charged." He fingered the ruffle at the end of her shirtsleeve. "Was there someone special?"

"Sort of."

The nerve along his jaw tightened—was he jealous of a man he'd never met? "Tell me about him," Jake insisted.

"His name was David. We dated my junior year of college. He was an English major and had planned on becoming a teacher."

"What happened?"

"I ended up pregnant."

Jake expelled a harsh breath. "You're a mother?"

She shook her head, and Jake ached for the pain glistening in her eyes. He sat up and tugged her near, wanting to offer comfort.

"I didn't even suspect I was pregnant when I snuck off on a ski trip with David. I collided with a tree on the slopes. Knocked myself silly. It wasn't until I was in the ER that I began cramping and ended up miscarrying. My parents were notified, and of course they were shocked and disappointed. My father had words with David."

"Guess David and I have something in common," Jake muttered, then added when Amanda frowned, "We both found ways to piss off your old man." *David got you pregnant and I discovered your old man in bed with my mother.*

"David broke up with me and transferred to a different school. Never heard from him again."

"I'm sorry about the baby, Amanda." He kissed her forehead.

"I always thought I'd make a good mother, but maybe it's not meant to be."

He lay back on the blanket, tucking Amanda against his side.

"Did you ever marry?" she asked.

"No."

"That's it?" She ruffled his hair. "Spill your guts, Turner, or I'm out of here."

He tightened his arms, daring her to wiggle free. "There were a couple of women in my past, but nothing serious."

"You're lying. A man as handsome as you…there had to have been one special lady."

"Whenever things got serious, I cut loose." He tilted her chin, forcing her to make eye contact. "At first, I believed my troubled relationship with my mom was the reason I couldn't commit to a relationship."

"That's understandable."

His gaze traveled over Amanda's face. "After a few failed affairs, I realized I couldn't give away something that wasn't in my possession to begin with."

"I don't understand."

Jake rolled Amanda to her back and rested his arms on either side of her. He traced her cheek with his fingertip. "Took me a while," he whispered, "to figure out I'd never gotten over you."

He held his breath, waiting for a signal to kiss her. He didn't intend to just tell her that he hadn't gotten over her—he wanted to show her.

She caressed his jaw, the side of his face, then ran her fingers through his hair to the back of his head where she pressed gently. He kissed her slow, easy and deep. The way he'd always dreamed of making love to her.

The first explosion rumbled through the sky, but Amanda's moan muffled the sound of the fireworks. One more, he decided, kissing her again…and again…and again.

Chapter Four

"You sure it's okay to park the Harley on your sidewalk?" Jake asked, shutting the front door behind him.

The drive home from the fireworks had been the longest ride of Amanda's life. Their make-out session had prompted her to suggest they leave Canyon Lake early. Jake's confession that he hadn't booked a motel room for the night had played into her plans. She had the bad boy right where she wanted him—in her house.

A little miffed he appeared more concerned with his motorcycle while she fretted over how to seduce him, she assured him, "The bike is fine." She ran her gaze over his body, her eyes stalling on the front of his tight jeans before continuing down the length of his thighs. Lord, the man could fill out a pair of button-fly 501's.

He cleared his throat, the rumble drawing her attention to his face. "I'll bunk on the couch."

The couch? Her heart sank. Had she read the signals wrong? *No.* She hadn't been the only one moaning on the blanket a short while ago. "Nonsense. You'll use the guest room." She had a better chance of enticing him into her bed if they slept on the same floor. Amanda resisted the urge to fidget under his solemn brown-eyed stare.

"If you're sure…"

Heck, yes, she was sure. She and Jake had almost made love the night before their high-school graduation, but for some reason—a reason she still didn't understand today—he'd changed his mind and put a stop to the caresses and kisses. After all these years of wondering what she'd missed out on, she was determined not to let Jake leave the house until they made love. "Follow me."

Upon reaching the second-floor landing, she pointed to the bathroom as she strolled past. "Fresh towels are in the cabinet." Then she paused at the guest-bedroom door. "There's space in the closet if you care to hang up anything."

"I'll get my clothes in the morning."

An image of Jake sleeping nude flashed through her mind and her pulse leaped. "Let me know if you need anything."

He tangled his fingers in her hair and tugged. Their noses bumped. Breath mingled. He nuzzled her lips—the barest of touches. "'Night, Amanda."

She hurried into her room and changed into her sexiest lingerie—a white cotton ankle-length nightgown with spaghetti straps. After slipping off her panties, she posed in front of the mirror. At least the material was sheer enough to see her silhouette underneath.

The bathroom door squeaked. Five minutes passed, then another squeak. She counted to ten before parading into the hall—and discovering he'd closed the bedroom door. *Drat.* She knocked softly. No answer. *Knock. Knock.* Again no answer. He couldn't have fallen asleep already. Frustrated, she rested her forehead against the door.

A moment later the door was yanked open and her forehead thumped Jake's naked chest. "What's wrong?" He grabbed her shoulders.

"Ah…" *Think!* "I thought you might be hungry." *For me.*

"Not really. See you in the morning." For the second time in less than ten minutes Jake Turner shut the door in her face.

"MORNIN'."

At the purr of Jake's sleep-slurred voice, Amanda tightened her fingers around the coffee cup she'd been rinsing. She'd intended to escape out the back door before he'd crawled from bed. Mentally swatting at the butterflies fluttering in her stomach, she dried her hands on a towel until every last drop of moisture disappeared, then faced her overnight guest.

Naked from the waist up, Jake lounged barefoot in the kitchen doorway. Amanda fought to keep her gaze from following the trail of dark hair that disappeared beneath the waistband of his unbuttoned jeans. She swallowed a sigh at his mussed state—hair sticking up, sleep creases branded into the side of his neck and beard stubble shadowing his cheeks. The sex god had spent the night under her roof and hadn't touched her. "Did you sleep well?" She forced a cheery note in her voice.

He raised his arms above his head to stretch, drawing Amanda's gaze to his bunching pectoral muscles. "The bed was too short."

Precisely. She'd anticipated that the twin mattress in the guest room would be uncomfortable and had hoped he'd crawl into bed with *her.* Amanda had tossed and turned all night, struggling to figure out where she'd gone wrong. His snub still stung and she was tempted to make him sleep on the porch tonight. "You should have curled up on your side," she teased.

"I prefer to sprawl."

Amanda's mouth went dry as she pictured Jake's body *sprawled* across the mattress. "I have to get to work. Help yourself to whatever's in the fridge." She retrieved her purse from the counter. "Coffee mugs are in the cupboard next to the sink." She was halfway to the door when Jake's voice stopped her.

"Don't I get a kiss?"

When she spun, he'd crossed the room. Planting his hands against the door frame above her head, he leaned forward, his gaze glued to her mouth. She focused on the sexy tuft of dark hair under his arm, afraid her eyes would betray her eagerness for his kiss. When he touched his lips to hers, she caught the faint scent of mint toothpaste. He nuzzled her cheek, then blew in her ear. "You smell good," he whispered before settling his mouth firmly over hers. The kiss didn't last long, but it warmed Amanda down to her toes and left her breathless.

When he pulled away, she said in a rush, "I get off at three, but I promised Miss Blanchard I'd help with the class-reunion registration at the Silver Palace until five."

"What time is the mixer tonight?" His chest brushed the front of her plum-colored silk blouse and her nipples perked.

The scent of his sleepy body made her dizzy and she was afraid she'd have to call in sick to work if she didn't move away from the man. When the screen door stood between them, she answered, "Seven. At the Ruby Slipper."

He grinned. "Have a good day, Ms. Brain."

Amanda walked on the narrow brick path alongside the house, then halted at the sight of the Harley parked next to the porch steps. *What will the neighbors think?* Too cranky to care, she skirted the bike and cut across the green patch of grass she called the front yard, and headed for the library three blocks away—a commute most people would kill for.

The vigorous walk worked off her frustration, and by the time she reached the corner of Main and Hesslinger she was ready to face anything—except Mrs. O'Reilly and Taco—her fifteen-pound Chihuahua.

"Hello, dear. I was on my way to your house. Betty phoned about a motorcycle parked in your yard." She shook her head. "I told the city council we should build a parking garage for tourists, but they don't listen to old people." She inched forward. "I'll call Deputy John. He'll help."

"That won't be necessary, Mrs. O'Reilly. The bike belongs

to Jake Turner. Remember Susan Turner's son? Jake and I went to high school together."

The old woman frowned. "He was a bit of a troublemaker, wasn't he?"

Poor Jake. Would he ever live down his bad-boy reputation? "I invited Jake to stay at my home while he's in town attending the weekend festivities."

Mrs. O'Reilly smacked her chest with an open palm. "But you're a single woman, dear."

"Rest assured my single status works better than a chastity belt. I tried to seduce Jake last night, but he'd have nothing to do with me." When the old biddy didn't hit the pavement in a dead faint, Amanda mumbled, "Have a good day, Mrs. O'Reilly."

Amanda had one foot in the library door when she was hit with the first question.

"Is it true?"

Already the wolves were circling. "Is what true?" Amanda growled at her coworker Kathy as she stored her purse in the desk drawer. She eyed the empty coffeemaker across the room.

"Silver Cliff's notorious bad boy spent the night under your roof?"

Oh. My. God.

Darn Mrs. O'Reilly and that new cell phone her kids had purchased for her this past Christmas. As if the woman and her overweight dog had nothing better to do than roam the streets reporting neighbors' comings and goings. Obviously the old biddy had contacted Martha, who worked in the library circulation department, who then told Bernice in the children's section, who in turn informed Kathy at the checkout desk. "You're twenty-three years old," Amanda argued. "How would you be aware of Jake's notoriety?"

Kathy shrugged. "I've heard his name around town. His mom died a few years ago, right? They said she was a drunk."

Amanda winced at the callous name-calling. Yes, Susan had been an alcoholic most of her life, but she'd also been a human being, with feelings, regrets, dreams and hopes.

"Jake slept at my house because the motels are booked solid for the class reunion."

"Yeah, right." Kathy followed Amanda to the coffeepot. "What was it like?"

"What was what like?"

"Sex with such a stud. I mean, a woman like you—"

"Like me?" Amanda set her coffee cup on the counter and gave the younger woman her best I'm-the-boss scowl.

Kathy retreated a step. "One who's not..." The bell at the front desk rang. "Experienced."

While the insult sank into Amanda's sleep-deprived brain, Kathy had dashed off. Amanda understood that people in town considered her a dried-up prune. And they were right. She was approaching forty and had had no more than a handful of dates the past ten years.

Pretty hair—that was what the girls at the Cut-Off Hair Salon assured her she had—and a lean figure were hardly enough to eliminate the stigma attached to her job—*librarian.* In a small-town dictionary, the word was synonymous with *old maid.*

If you're not an old maid, then what are you?

A coward. She should have marched into Jake's bedroom and jumped his bones. Last night she'd lied to herself, maintaining the reason she'd wanted to have sex with Jake was to discover what she'd missed out on all those years ago. But one look at him this morning—groggy and sexy as all get out—and she'd realized that her feelings for him in high school had withstood a twenty-year separation.

Amanda yearned for more than great sex with Jake. She wanted a future. If only she had more than two days to make Jake believe he couldn't live without her.

"Amanda," Kathy called from the front desk. "Deputy John wishes to speak with you."

Oh, brother. "Hello, John." Amanda greeted the tall, pencil-thin officer after exiting her office. Kathy slunk off to the children's section and resumed her patron-spying post behind the Dr. Seuss display.

"Change your mind about being a guest reader?" she asked. Three months ago she'd invited John to read a story on bike safety to Valerie's day-care kids. She hadn't realized John stuttered when he read out loud. The poor man had acted as if he'd rather face down a serial killer than a group of preschoolers.

"Mrs. O'Reilly reported a motorcycle parked at your house." He rested his hand over the butt of his gun as if the perpetrator lurked between the shelves of books.

Amanda leaned forward and whispered, "Settle down, Barney Fife. Jake Turner isn't here."

John had the grace to blush. "Is he causing problems?"

Not the kind I can talk about publicly.

The deputy had been a freshman when Amanda and Jake were seniors. "Jake is not harassing me." No wonder Jake had stayed away from Silver Cliff all these years. "I explained to Mrs. O'Reilly that I'd invited Jake to sleep over." At the cop's bug-eyed gape, she added, "In the guest bedroom."

"Mrs. O'Reilly is concerned that Turner may not have your best interests—"

"John. Do I look like someone who would let herself be taken advantage of?"

"Ah, no."

Well, shoot. Maybe that was the problem. She'd have to phone Valerie. As a former hooker, she could probably give Amanda a few pointers. "I appreciate that Mrs. O'Reilly is concerned, but it's none of her business who I allow in my home."

Remember, Amanda, you work with children. That gives adults the right to scrutinize your personal life—to a certain extent. She supposed rumors that she and Jake were having a torrid affair might compromise her good standing—a chance she was willing to accept.

"I agree that it's none of Mrs. O'Reilly's business," John admitted. "Just the same, if Turner steps over the line, call the station, and I'll be right over."

Steps over the line... Tonight she hoped Jake would leap across the line and let loose his bad-boy ways on her.

Chapter Five

The Silver Palace hadn't changed much over the years—it was still the same swanky hotel that Jake's mother had argued their kind wasn't welcome inside. From his vantage point across the street, he spotted the three mammoth crystal chandeliers visible behind the towering paned windows at the front of the building. Yep, all ritz and glitz.

He checked his watch: 5:00 p.m. Fifteen minutes ago, he'd caught a glimpse of Amanda strolling through the lobby. He'd thought about her a lot today. Found himself missing her…counting the hours until she got off work.

The desire to learn everything about her had driven him to wander through her house and take inventory of her possessions. Her favorite color was pink. Bath towels. Coffee cups. Throw pillows. Even the good china boasted a pink-flowered pattern. Pink suited Amanda. The color represented the soft, safe side of her that Jake ached to lose himself in.

He'd studied the collection of old family photographs she'd displayed on the foyer table and had wondered what the preacher would say if he'd discovered Jake had slept under his daughter's roof last night.

The hotel blurred before Jake's eyes as a memory formed in his mind: walking into his house after school and catching Amanda's father having sex with his mother in the bedroom.

His mother—head turned toward the wall, eyes vacant. Her body lifeless. The preacher moving over her like a rutting animal.

Jake had fled the room unnoticed and waited outside. When the preacher stepped onto the porch, Jake had expected the man to show regret. Embarrassment. Maybe even fear. But not indifference.

"I was sharing the word of the Lord with your mother," the man had boasted, tucking his shirt into his pants.

"People at church care you're spreading God's word through your…?" Jake had meant to anger and provoke, but the vulgar question produced only a patronizing smile from the preacher.

"Son, God is a forgiving man. If you'd attend church, you'd understand that."

The idea that Amanda's father believed he wasn't accountable to anyone but the person in the sky had angered Jake. *"God might forgive you, but people won't."*

"Talk all you want, boy. No one will believe you. Your mother's a drunk. And we both know I'm not the first man to visit her bedroom. Nor will I be the last."

The truth hit Jake hard. For the first time in his life he'd understood how the poor and less fortunate were discounted by society. He and his mother were of little value, therefore they didn't deserve to be treated with the same respect as others. *You'll pay for this,* he'd muttered as the preacher drove away.

Little had Jake expected the opportunity for revenge would land in his lap a few days later when Amanda had offered her tutoring services. In the end, though, Jake's feelings had gotten in the way of going through with his plan to seduce Amanda.

After Jake had explored the rest of Amanda's house, he'd sat outside at the iron tea table in the backyard, surrounded by decorative birdhouses, birdbaths and pots of flowers, and thought about how his childhood had been so opposite Amanda's. He'd expected to return to Silver Cliff and discover they had nothing in common. How wrong he'd been. Even though they both had fulfilling careers and friendships, their lives were missing something—or rather, that special someone. Amanda should have been a mother by now, yet she lived alone, not even a steady boyfriend. And Jake had never become serious with any of the women he'd dated in the past.

Everything in him shouted Amanda was *the one*. He wondered if she had any inkling how difficult it had been to ignore her invitation last night. He'd tossed and turned in bed, fighting the temptation to crawl beneath her big pink comforter, wrap her in his arms and free himself in her sweetness. But he couldn't. The past—rather, Amanda's father—stood between them.

But was telling the truth the answer? The truth would hurt Amanda. Forever change her relationship with her father. Besides, her life was in Silver Cliff and his was in L.A. If Amanda had no intention of ever moving away, then why tell her the truth?

Because you could move here. Make a life with Amanda in Silver Cliff. Her father wasn't around. His mother was dead. They could make it work.

A computer and a cell phone were all he required to run his software company. He'd have to relocate the commuter jet to the Silver Cliff Regional Airport twelve miles outside of town in order to attend meetings once a month in L.A. Money made anything possible, except for one thing—wealth couldn't buy acceptance. Jake wasn't sure he'd be welcomed back to Silver Cliff by its residents—not that they could stop him from moving here. But he had to consider Amanda.

If they became a couple, how would the locals treat her? Would she keep her job? Her friends? He'd been an outcast all his life and he'd never wish for Amanda to suffer the same fate.

Silver Cliff was more Amanda's town than his and he had no intention of jeopardizing her good standing. But that didn't mean he couldn't test the waters—get a feel for how people would react to seeing them as a couple.

Had she missed him as much as he'd missed her today? Would her face light up when he strolled through the huge hotel doors? Before he lost his courage, he crossed the street and entered the Silver Palace.

A small crowd gathered near the mahogany check-in desk. Several in the group stared, but he resisted the urge to dive behind the potted palm near the front window. His mother hadn't lied. The placed oozed wealth—ornate carpets, plush ivory-colored couches and chairs, even a pianist playing a baby grand.

"Jake, over here."

His heart beat double time when he spotted Amanda waving from across the lobby. Her hair wasn't as neat as it had been in the morning and wrinkles creased the front of her skirt, but she was the prettiest woman in the whole world. Unable to drag his eyes from her tousled state, he headed in her direction. They met in front of a massive white column on the far side of the lobby. She coaxed him behind the pillar into a dimly lit alcove.

"I missed you," she murmured, curling her arms around his neck.

"How much?" His hands greedily clutched her hips.

"This much." Her breath fanned his face as her mouth inched upward.

Jake resisted the urge to take control, to kiss her the way he'd fantasized about all day—hard and hot. Lots of tongue. Soft and tentative, she flirted with his mouth. "More," he breathed. "Way more." When she ran her tongue over his lower lip, Jake's knees damn near gave out.

Tangling a hand in her hair, he pressed a bruising kiss to

her mouth. *Sweet. So sweet.* He wanted his kiss to say everything he couldn't—that he ached for a future with her, that he ached to be her everything, that he yearned to fit into her world. When they finally came up for air, he pulled Amanda close, marveling at the perfect fit of their bodies.

"I didn't expect you to stop by," she whispered.

"Your house is boring. No big-screen TV. No satellite dish. No video-game system," he teased.

"And here I thought you'd be racing your Harley through the mountains all day."

"No fun without you on the back." He lowered his head and she met him halfway. The urgency having been sated with the first kiss, he took his time—little nibbles and long easy strokes of the tongue.

"Ahem."

Jake and Amanda jumped apart at the throat-clearing sound. A few feet away an older woman smiled.

"Miss Blanchard, you remember Jake Turner, don't you?" Amanda discreetly wiped the back of her hand across her wet-slicked lips. "Jake, I believe Miss Blanchard taught English your senior year."

"I remember you, young man. You earned a solid B in my class." She held out her hand.

Jake wasn't sure what to do with that hand, but he clasped it in both of his and said, "Nice to see you, Miss Blanchard." His attempt to remove his hand was met with resistance.

"I wouldn't believe it possible, but you've grown more handsome with time."

Uncertain what to make of the teacher's flirtatious remark, Jake mumbled, "Thank you, ma'am."

"I was delighted to hear you'd returned for the reunion. I understand you're staying with Amanda."

Evidently his shacking up with the town librarian was public knowledge. Was it possible that Amanda wasn't bothered by his past and what people thought about him as much as he was? "The hotels were booked and she was nice enough to loan me her couch."

Miss Blanchard's smile dimmed. "I'm sorry to hear that. I had expected…well, never mind."

Expected? Expected what—that he and Amanda would have sex?

"I'd better resume my duties, but I wanted to be sure to say hello." The retired teacher walked off, calling over her shoulder, "I hope you've come home to stay, Jake."

Home to stay… If the English teacher welcomed Jake back, would others, as well? Tonight at the Ruby Slipper, Silver Cliff's once historical brothel, he'd discover how welcome he was.

"Is THAT Jake Turner?" Kelly Smith asked, joining Amanda in the bar of the Ruby Slipper. Kelly, former Class of '87 president, was a feature reporter for KCNC news in Denver. Pretty, smart and tonight sexy in a little black dress that appeared as if it had been airbrushed onto her. There was nothing to find fault with in Kelly—except the sparkle of interest in her eyes as she studied Jake. Clad in black jeans and a mustard-colored mock turtleneck, Jake was the sexiest man in the saloon.

"Back off, Hollywood," Amanda warned, using Kelly's high-school nickname. Then she added with a sugary smile, "Jake's my date."

"Really?"

"Really." Why was it difficult for others to believe a man as handsome as Jake might be interested in her, the local librarian?

"How long have you two been an item?" Kelly probed.

Amanda checked her wristwatch. "Almost twenty-nine hours."

Two perfectly plucked eyebrows arched. "Not long."

"Long enough," Amanda grumbled. She glanced at her red

dress, wondering if she was properly equipped to declare war against the brunette. She couldn't compete with Kelly's *Penthouse* figure, but appreciation had shown on Jake's face earlier in the evening when Amanda had appeared in the sequined dress.

"Are you two involved in a whirlwind affair?"

I wish. Although tempted, Amanda refused to lie. Jake had been on the receiving end of rumors his entire life and she wouldn't contribute to the gossip. "I'm loaning him my couch for the weekend."

"Ah-ha. Fair game, then," Kelly murmured.

Amanda chose to pretend she hadn't heard the comment as she watched Jake head toward them. She'd never seen a man so confident. He wasn't the same troubled kid who'd blown out of town twenty years ago.

"Hello, Kelly." Jake stopped next to Amanda and set his hand on her lower back. Aware of Kelly's envious stare, Amanda snuggled against his side. Maybe there was hope he wouldn't fall under Hollywood's spell.

"Hello, Jake. You look…great." Kelly's eyes did the roaming thing again and Amanda wanted to stomp on the toe of the flirt's three-inch-heeled shoe.

Amanda appreciated that Jake hadn't returned the "looking…great" sentiment, and if Kelly had noticed, she didn't let on. "What do you do for a living?" Kelly inquired.

The question sent a rush of heat up Amanda's neck and she fanned herself with a cocktail napkin.

"You okay?" Jake grasped her elbow.

"It's a little warm in here," she muttered. What must Jake think? She'd spent the past two days with him and hadn't bothered to ask what he did for a living. Had he assumed she wasn't interested, or, worse, that she didn't care? He probably believed she was shallow, and that was why he hadn't jumped into bed with her.

"I own a software company," he answered.

Really?

"Really?" Kelly echoed Amanda's thought. "You're a math and computers guy."

Hardly. Jake hated math. Amanda had managed to help him eke out a C in Algebra II his senior year…barely.

Jake shook his head. "I despise math, but I love computers. My business partner is a genius programmer."

"What's the name of your company?"

"JT Communications, Inc."

"JT…Jake Turner." Kelly snapped her fingers. "Virus-protection software. The TV station did a feature story on your product, but they didn't interview you. They talked with a company spokesperson."

Left out of the conversation, Amanda swallowed the lump in her throat and again wondered how she could not have asked Jake how he made his income. He knew everything about her and she knew zip, *nada,* nothing about his life outside Silver Cliff.

"My senior programmer is currently working on the next generation of computer security," Jake added. "She's brilliant."

She. The lump grew larger until Amanda's throat threatened to swell shut. She was nothing but a dull librarian. Hardly as exciting as Jake's brilliant female computer programmer.

"Ted, over here." Kelly waved at a man in the crowd. "You remember Ted Butler. He graduated a year ahead of us. Manages a motel chain in Vegas." When the short, rotund man joined the group, Kelly said, "Ted, this is Jake Turner of JT Communications."

Amanda waited for her introduction, but it never materialized. As a conversation in wireless security ensued, the circle closed and Amanda found herself standing on the outside. And here she'd been worried that Jake would have trouble fitting in tonight. Feeling sorry for herself, she roamed over to the bar. "A shot of tequila, barkeep," she ordered, sliding onto an empty stool.

The bartender handed Amanda a shot glass of liquor, a slice of lemon and a saltshaker. She studied the items, then shrugged. She sprinkled salt over the lemon, then squeezed until juice dribbled into the tequila.

"It appears that Ms. Brain needs a tutor," Jake whispered near her ear, his hot breath rustling her hair.

She stuck out her lower lip. "My tequila tutor *appears* more interested in talking than teaching."

"No way, babe." He bent his head and kissed her. Not a little peck. Not a sisterly smooch. A man-to-woman *kiss* that curled her toes and told anyone watching that Amanda belonged to Jake. "Now, pay attention." He clenched his hand into a fist, ran his tongue across the skin below his index finger and sprinkled salt over the area. Then he licked off the salt, tossed back the tequila in one swallow and bit into the lemon wedge.

"You're good." His eyes didn't even water.

"Practice makes perfect." He motioned for the bartender to bring another round. "Your turn."

Amanda followed his instructions, a bit slower, and succeeded in downing the tequila in two swallows. Her eyes watered. "My throat is on fire," she wheezed.

"The second shot won't burn as much."

Within a few minutes, a small crowd had gathered around Amanda and Jake. Shot glasses were lined up along the length of the bar. Saltshakers appeared, and lemon and lime wedges passed around.

"Ready...set...go!" someone shouted.

Amanda swallowed the tequila in one gulp, then immediately coughed. "Third time's a charm." Jake grinned. "Line 'em up, barkeep," he ordered.

"I think I'm getting drunk, Jake," Amanda mumbled, her stomach warming from the liquor.

"I'll make sure you get home tonight, even if I have to carry you."

The image of Jake slinging the local librarian over his shoulder and hauling her inebriated fanny through the streets brought a smile to Amanda's face.

The good folks of Silver Cliff would be talking about Amanda Winslow's tequila-shooter lesson for years to come.

Chapter Six

"One more step," Jake coaxed, half lugging, half pushing Amanda up the front porch.

Her heel caught on the top step and her arms windmilled. "Whoa!" She toppled backward into Jake.

After glancing around, he scooped her up and carried her to the door. At one in the morning, the block was dark, save for Amanda's porch light, which splashed their monster-size silhouettes against the house. "The key," he urged, hoping none of the neighbors was spying on them.

Ms. Brain wasn't so much inebriated as she was exhausted. She'd stopped after four tequila shooters and chugged coffee the rest of the evening. But after a long day of work and several turns on the dance floor with him and others, she was done in.

"Right here." She lifted her beaded purse, accidentally whacking Jake across the head. "Oops." She struggled with the zipper.

"Let me." His big fingers dug through the dainty clutch. After confiscating the key, he opened the lock, carried Amanda inside and kicked the door closed with his boot heel.

He considered setting her on her feet but decided he preferred her right where she was—snuggled against his chest. Hoisting her high in his arms, he climbed the stairs to the second floor. In the hallway he propped her against the wall outside the bathroom and sucked in several deep breaths.

Her fingers toyed with his ear. "You're out of shape."

Maybe he should change his exercise routine—heck of a lot cheaper and more fun to tote Amanda around than to shell out big bucks for a membership at the athletic club. Before he admitted as much, he heard a sniffle. *A sniffle?* He tilted her chin, stunned at the tears glistening in her pretty eyes. "What's wrong?"

"I'm sorry."

"Sorry for what?"

"That I never asked about your job." A liquid drop leaked from the corner of her eye and dribbled down her cheek.

Frowning, he insisted, "It's not import—"

She cut him off. "All these years, you've been so success-ful."

"Yeah, well, don't get any ideas about calling me *brain*," he joked, hoping to lighten the mood.

"You never returned, Jake." Her lower lip wobbled.

Oh, boy. The real reason behind the tears. "Please stop crying." He kissed her cheek, which led to kissing her chin, which led to exploring her collarbone after he slid aside the dress's shoulder strap.

A warm purr vibrated in her throat. She wrapped her arms around his neck and tangled her fingers in his hair. Their hot mouths mated, his tongue campaigning for a part of his anatomy that ached to get in on the action. After lengthy ex-ploration, he ended the kiss and rested his forehead against hers. "I've been dying to do that ever since I saw you in—" he tugged the hem of her dress "—this little number."

"Really?" Her breath puffed against his face. "I thought you preferred Kelly's little black number."

"Nope. *Red* is definitely my color." And maybe green. His ego appreciated Amanda's jealous bone. "There's something else I've been dreaming of doing." He cupped her breast in his palm and squeezed. "This." The feel of her was pure heaven. Touching wasn't enough. "I want you, Amanda." Intending for there to be no mistake about the definition of *want,* he thrust his erection against her thigh and groaned.

"Yes." She nibbled his jaw. "Yes, yes, yes."

Blood racing, he bent at the knees and scooped her into his arms, questioning why he'd ever put her down in the first place. Inside the bedroom he laid her on the pink ruffled comforter and stretched out beside her. "I've thought about making love to you on this frilly bed since the fireworks last night." He nuzzled her neck.

"Wait." Her fingertips flexed against his shoulders.

Concerned by the wobble in her voice, he levered himself onto his elbows. Her blue eyes were huge, almost too big for her face. "What's wrong? Change of heart?" He sure in hell hoped not.

"I've always wondered why you didn't make love to me that night in my bedroom."

Swallowing a groan, Jake rolled away and sat on the edge of the bed. He shoved a hand through his hair, silently cursing. He didn't care to discuss the past. Not now. Maybe not ever.

Amanda moved behind him and wrapped her arms around his waist, then rested her cheek against his shoulder. "Was it because of my father?"

Yes.

"Because I was the preacher's daughter?"

Yes. "Amanda, let's not discuss—"

"You owe me an explanation."

He could give her part of the truth. "I didn't make love to you because I realized that my feelings for you had altered."

Her arms fell away, but he grabbed her hands and held them tight to his chest. "It wasn't supposed to happen. I fought it. But in the end I couldn't stop myself from caring about you." *Loving you.*

"I don't understand. If you—"

"I would have hurt you," he blurted louder than he'd intended.

She scooted to the side. "Hurt me how?"

Jake admitted there was a small part of him—a part he was ashamed of—that yearned to destroy the man who'd preyed upon his mother—a weak woman lost in despair. But revenge wasn't worth risking the chance of a future with Amanda. He left the bed and moved across the room. "I wasn't the kind of guy a girl like you should have been involved with."

"I was aware my father disapproved of you. In fact, he threatened to ground me for life if I didn't quit tutoring you."

"Why did you chance your father's wrath to help me?"

"I wanted everyone in our class to graduate." Then she smiled. "And I thought you were cute."

Her honesty caught him off guard and he chuckled. "Cute?"

"Okay, not cute. You were a stud." Her expression sobered. "After we became better acquainted, I began to like you and then…like turned to love."

"Love?" Was she serious? "You never told me."

"How could I when you never said how you felt about me? That night in my bedroom I was gathering the courage to tell you, but then you went all weird and left."

He doubted Amanda's confession would have influenced his actions that night. He'd been so confused, hurt and angry and had wondered if his feelings for Amanda had been genuine or anchored in the hate he'd felt for her father. "I left because I refused to cause trouble between you and your father."

Compassion filled her gaze. "I understand your life wasn't easy in Silver Cliff. But once my father got to know you and your mother, he would have recognized that you were good people. He would have approved of you and me."

She was delusional. But he didn't have the heart to shatter her perception of her father. "No, he wouldn't have."

"He's a preacher, Jake. He sees past the labels that society places on people," she argued.

"Are you sure about that?" Jake challenged, regretting the comment when her eyes widened in shock.

"What makes you so positive my father wouldn't have accepted you?"

"Never mind." He slipped his feet into his shoes.

"Jake, did my father hurt you?"

"Let it go, Amanda." He had to leave before he said something he regretted.

Amanda leaped from the bed. "You're not doing this to me again."

"Doing what?"

"Running away."

"I'm not running away. I just need some air."

"What did my father do?"

Her plea stopped him at the doorway. "Jake, wait. Please."

His chest ached at the tears streaming down her face. Once again, he'd hurt her. Maybe that was all he was capable of offering—pain.

"You're not leaving town, are you?"

"I don't—"

"Promise me you won't go without saying goodbye."

Did he dare?

"Promise, Jake," she whispered fiercely.

"I promise." He fled the house, hopped on his Harley and sped off into the darkness, not caring that the rev of the bike engine woke the neighbors. Or that Amanda, with her heart aching, stood in the shadows of the bedroom window, watching the taillights of the Harley disappear into the darkness.

JAKE APPROACHED the edge of the crowd gathered near the entrance of Silver Cliff High School. He wasn't interested in the school-dedication ceremony, but he couldn't decide where to go after waking up this morning from a makeshift bed on the cold, hard ground outside the remains of his childhood home. With no shower and still wearing last night's clothes, he was certain he resembled something dragged from the depths of Canyon Lake.

He'd blown it with Amanda. Maybe it was for the best. Sooner or later the truth would come out. He didn't want Amanda to have to choose between him and her father. And then there remained the possibility that she'd wonder if his love for her had been real or if he'd just used her to avenge his mother. His and Amanda's past was too convoluted to straighten out or make sense of.

He'd do the noble thing and walk away. Walk away from the one woman who'd given him the very things he'd hungered for all his life—acceptance. Respect. Love.

Jake's thoughts were interrupted when Mayor Mike Passky tapped his fingers against the microphone. A chorus of groans followed the ear-piercing screech emitted by the sound system.

"Ladies and gentlemen and former Soaring Eagle students. It is with great pride that we gather today on the steps of this historic building. Silver Cliff High opened its doors in 1927 and has proudly served the community for eighty years." Jake half listened to the mayor drone on about the institution's history and its teachers. He didn't care that the classrooms would be converted into condos for the wealthy.

"Hello, Jake."

Jake tensed, then steeled himself and turned. Milton Mahoney, former principal of the high school. A man whose one mission had been to make Jake's life miserable.

"Mahoney," Jake muttered.

Life had not treated the old man well. Only a handful of gray hair sprouted from his head. Mahoney's eyelids and jowls sagged, and the lightweight sport coat hung on his frame like a tarp instead of a fitted jacket. Time and age had eliminated Mahoney's threatening authority, but not Jake's hard feelings toward the man.

"I'm sorry about your mother."

The unexpected condolence caught Jake by surprise. "Thanks."

An uncomfortable silence ensued while Jake focused on the mayor's accolades of the developer who'd purchased the school. Hell, the last place Jake would ever consider living was inside a classroom, but he supposed a sense of nostalgia appealed to some people.

Irritated that Mahoney didn't walk off, Jake grumbled, "If you're worried about me sticking around town, don't. I'm heading out shortly." As soon as he said a final goodbye to Amanda.

"Wait. I owe you an apology."

The ex-principal never apologized. *Ever.* "What for?"

"For the way I treated you in high school."

Memories of the man humiliating Jake in front of other students hadn't lost their sting with the passing of years. He'd been told countless times that he would never amount to much in life.

Mahoney grabbed Jake's arm and coaxed him away from the crowd. "There's no excuse for my actions over the years, but I assure you it was nothing personal."

"Felt damn personal to me."

"I took out my anger at your mother on you," Mahoney admitted.

"What does my mother have to do with anything?" First the preacher, now the principal?

"I was fresh out of college and a new teacher at the high school when your mother was a senior. I fell in love with her on sight and she loved me. At least in the beginning."

Jake had difficultly envisioning his mother with a jerk like Mahoney.

"We couldn't date, of course, but we found ways to be together. I bought an engagement ring and intended to propose after she graduated."

That Mahoney had once cared for his mother made the preacher's treatment of her even more unforgivable. Not sure he wanted to hear the sordid details of a failed love affair between his mother and his former principal, Jake assured the man, "You don't owe me an explanation."

With an expression of utter wretchedness, Mahoney begged, "Yes, I do."

Unable to resist the pathetic plea, Jake nodded.

"The week before your mother's graduation, your father drifted into town. I'm not sure where Susan met him, but he turned her head. She broke things off with me before I had the chance to propose. At the end of the summer, your father left. A few weeks later Susan discovered she was pregnant with you. I offered to marry her. To give you my name and raise you as my son. She refused, believing that your father would return to marry her."

Jake finished the story. "But he never came back."

"He showed up a few months after you were born. Stayed around until your first birthday, then skipped town. To my knowledge that was the last time your mother ever saw him. I waited a few months to propose again. She said she refused to marry a man she couldn't love."

But she could sleep with men she didn't love.

"Then Susan began drinking and I hated your father even more for what he'd done to her." Mahoney cleared his throat. "You look like him." The lines bracketing Mahoney's mouth deepened with sorrow. "Every time I saw your face, I was reminded of the man who stole Susan from me. I'm sorry, Jake. More sorry than you'll ever understand for taking out my hurt and anger on you."

Jake wasn't sure what to say to Mahoney. The man had lived

his entire life loving a woman who couldn't return his. Jake needed time to digest the information, but he felt compelled to offer the former principal an olive branch. "I'm sorry it didn't work out, but I'm glad you loved my mother. Glad someone did."

"She'd be very proud of you and what you've done with your life."

"Thank you."

"I understand you've been escorting Amanda Winslow to the reunion events." When Jake snorted, Mahoney added, "Not much stays private in this town."

"Tell me about it."

"You two have a fight?"

"You're kidding, right?"

Mahoney shrugged. "Deputy John stopped in at the Breakfast Mill and mentioned that a neighbor of Amanda's called in a noise complaint about a loud motorcycle. You're the only one in town with a Harley." Mahoney's gaze roamed over Jake. "Looks like you slept in your clothes."

"I did."

"You're welcome to shower and get ready at my place for the dinner tonight."

Jake stared at Mahoney as though he couldn't believe he was having this conversation with the man who'd had it out for him all through high school. He rubbed the stubble on his face and considered the offer.

He pictured Amanda attending the reunion dinner all alone. Sitting single at a table full of doubles. Maybe forever wasn't in the cards for them. But before leaving town, he would be her escort this evening, and if she wished to live with the memory, he'd give her the night of lovemaking she'd waited twenty long years for.

"Thanks, Mahoney. I'll take you up on your offer."

Chapter Seven

6:01 p.m.

He's not coming. Amanda paced the front hallway, debating whether to leave for the hotel or wait ten more minutes in the hope that Jake would show up.

The phone had rung off the hook all day. Valerie wanted to know if she and Jake had broken up—as if they'd been a couple in the first place. Deputy John advised her that a neighbor had reported a commotion last night—Jake revving the Harley engine as he'd sped off. Miss Blanchard suggested her nephew escort Amanda to the dinner and dance—assuming Jake intended to stand her up. And several more calls from her nosy library staff, collecting fodder for the gossip mill.

When the phone had ceased ringing, Amanda had attempted to make sense of what had transpired between her and Jake the previous evening. What should have been a night of enchanted lovemaking had ended with Jake walking out the front door. She analyzed their conversation over and over and arrived at one conclusion: her father had been the reason Jake had fled town following their graduation ceremony. The idea that her father's actions had affected Jake so deeply he'd held on to the memory all these years made Amanda both furious and sad.

She'd never expected Jake to waltz back into her life, and

refused to watch him ride out of town a second time without putting up a fight. But she couldn't wage a battle against something she didn't understand—which left her no choice but to confront the source of the conflict.

After an extremely uncomfortable phone conversation with her father, Amanda had hung up and cried. Cried for Jake and the pain, anger and humiliation he'd carried inside him all these years. Cried for Susan, a troubled woman with a beautiful soul who'd been used in such a cruel way. Cried for her mother, who was to this day unaware of her husband's betrayal. Cried for her father, who was deeply remorseful for his actions and would one day have to answer to his highest critic. And last, she'd cried for the loss of what might have been and what might never be between her and Jake.

She was under no illusion that rehashing the past would fix things between her and Jake. But if Jake was half the man she believed him to be, then he'd allow her the courtesy of speaking her mind. Now all she had to do was pray he'd show up tonight so she had the opportunity to convince him that together they could overcome the past and reach for the future they both deserved.

The rumble of a motorcycle engine disrupted Amanda's thoughts. *Thank you, God.* She closed her eyes against the sting of tears and pulled in several deep breaths as anxiety gave way to relief. Until this moment she hadn't wished to admit how worried she'd been that Jake had skipped town without saying goodbye.

A sober face greeted her when she opened the door. He wore a one-button designer tux that had been tailored to fit his physique and had probably cost five times as much as her dress. Tonight, his dark hair was slicked back, lending him a rakish air. Only Amanda understood that the handsome exterior hid a tortured soul.

"Hi." She swallowed past the lump in her throat.

"You look gorgeous." His gaze caressed her body, from her upswept hairdo to the tips of her French-manicured toenails.

"Thank you." Fingering the knee-length hem, she added, "It's a Marilyn Monroe—"

"The Seven Year Itch," he interrupted. "The famous movie where she stands over a New York City subway grate, her dress blowing up around her waist." One brow rose suggestively.

"Shame on you," she scolded with a smile. "What would people say if the town librarian flipped up her dress in public?"

"That she's got the sexiest legs west of the Rocky Mountains."

"You're a terrible flirt." She motioned to the florist's box he held. "You bought me a corsage."

"I've always wanted to escort a girl to a school dance." He shrugged as if embarrassed by the confession.

Keeping her eyes on the white tea roses arranged around a wristband, she asked, "Why didn't you?" *I would have said yes.*

"The girl I would have liked to ask to the prom wasn't allowed to go with a boy like me."

Her heart ached at how much hurt her father had caused them both. "Come inside."

Amanda searched for a pair of scissors to open the florist box while Jake lounged in the kitchen doorway. "Did Stephie Dalton help you pick this out?" Stephie had graduated in their high-school class and was the owner of the town's sole flower shop.

"I believe she was upset that I didn't recognize her right away with those fake boobs and big hair." Jake grinned.

"She's not so bad once you get to know her." Rather than talking about Stephie, Amanda yearned to ask Jake where he'd slept last night. What he'd done all day. But she slipped the corsage over her wrist, grabbed her beaded clutch from the counter and sent a smile that promised all was well. "Ready."

Riding the Harley was out of the question unless Amanda intended to show off her new red satin panties to all the reunion attendees. They walked the six blocks to the posh hotel. The conversation was sporadic—"Nice weather this evening." "They flew the steak in fresh for tonight's menu." "Did you know the mayor is an ex-DJ?"

By the time they entered the main ballroom of the Silver Palace, Amanda worried that it might be too late for her and Jake.

"What can I get for you from the bar?" he inquired.

"A glass of white wine, please."

"No shooters tonight?"

"I believe I've had enough shooters for a while," she told him in her best librarian voice.

After Jake walked off to the cash bar, Amanda took a moment to appreciate the extravagant decorations boasting their school's colors: red, black and silver. The developer who'd purchased Silver Cliff High School surely helped foot the bill for such an extravagant party.

The table centerpieces were interestingly gaudy—definitely Stephie Dalton's handiwork. Rising from silver ice buckets loaded with fake silver nuggets were three-foot soaring eagle-shaped topiaries made of tiny white and black roses. Each bird held a red tulip in its mouth. A small stuffed mountain lion—the new school mascot—sat at each place setting, along with a souvenir silver-eagle napkin ring. Silver helium balloons floated from the center of the hundred and twenty-five tables, creating a starry-night atmosphere, and an elegant soaring-eagle ice sculpture graced the large banquet table at the back of the room.

Jake returned with her wine. "Thad and Valerie invited us to join them."

"Sure." Amanda weaved through the crowd, Jake behind her with a hand on her lower back. He was aware of the envious female glances following them. A surge of pride filled her at the thought that Jake was with *her* tonight and not any of the other gorgeous women milling about the room. They seated themselves at Thad and Valerie's table, then Mayor Passky approached the podium on the stage. After his brief welcoming speech, lines formed at all three buffet tables.

Although the conversation with their table guests was enjoyable, Amanda caught Jake's growing unease as the dinner progressed. Surreptitiously she studied the reunion attendees at nearby tables and noticed for the first time the hushed conversations marked with pointed stares at Jake. Most of the reunion attendees didn't even know Jake, but had probably heard about his past through the Silver Cliff grapevine, his successful software company and their *spat* last night. Feeling edgy, she set her napkin aside and uttered in Jake's ear, "Let's go."

Startled, he asked, "Now?"

"I'm not feeling well." Her stomach was a queasy ball of knots. She turned to Valerie and said, "I'll call you tomorrow." Then, ignoring her friend's stunned expression, Amanda stood and Jake escorted her from the room amid a bevy of craned-neck stares.

In the lobby, he touched her forehead in a tender gesture. "You don't feel feverish."

"I'm fine." She inched closer. "I just want to be alone with you."

He flashed a cocky grin. "In the mood for a ride on my Harley?"

"If we can race Switchback Mountain."

"What about the dance at the high school?" he asked.

Time was the enemy. Every minute…second counted. "I'd rather spend the rest of the evening dancing alone with you."

The heat in Jake's eyes promised Amanda a *dance* she'd never forget.

THERE WAS SOMETHING sexy and exciting about riding a Harley with a dress on. The powerful engine throbbed between Amanda's thighs, arousing her. She clung to Jake as the motorcycle dipped low around a hairpin curve three miles outside town. The cool evening air wrecked her upswept hairdo, whipping the blond strands across her face, and her red dress billowed, the night air caressing her naked legs.

After Jake straightened out the bike and accelerated on a straightaway, he stroked the sensitive flesh on the inside of her knee with his thumb. Stimulated by the touch…eager for more, she smashed her breasts to his back and nuzzled the crook of his neck. He growled, the sound in his throat vibrating against her mouth.

"Hang on," he shouted at the next sharp curve. No wonder high-school kids loved Switchback Mountain. The road, comprising curves and straightaways, could pass for a James Dean movie set. Jake slowed the bike's speed and she soaked up the ambience of the twilight ride.

"I want you." She spoke the word against his ear, then slid her tongue inside. She might have been mistaken, but she swore Jake and not the Harley rumbled in response to her boldness.

After a half mile Jake exited onto a mining road that led to the infamous Pecos Silver Mine. The silver mine had shut down in 1889 and only the crumbling remains of a handful of outbuildings dotted the landscape. Although the main entrance to the mine had been boarded up, the area was a favorite party place for local teenagers.

Several years before Amanda had graduated, a student had been crushed to death after he'd knocked loose a support beam in one of the interior chambers. After the incident, local authorities dynamited the remaining chambers and tunnels, leaving only the large cavern-like entrance.

Jake stopped the bike, then hopped off and held out a hand

to assist her. She swung a leg over the seat, aware she offered Jake an eyeful of red satin panty. Dusk had enveloped the mountains, turning the smattering of trees along the ridge into hulking shadows.

She and Jake stood for a moment, soaking up the quiet… each other…the knowledge of what they were about to share. Yearning wavered between them and Amanda thought her knees would give out if Jake didn't take her in his arms.

The first kiss was tentative, as if he didn't trust her not to change her mind. His vulnerability touched her, yet the knowledge that she possessed such feminine power over him emboldened her response. She clasped his face between her hands. "I want you, Jake Turner."

"Amanda. I have to tell you something and it might change the way you feel about—"

She rubbed her fingertips across his lips. "I love you. I fell in love with you the moment I entered the detention room and you tried to frighten me with your scowl." She gazed into his brown eyes, willing him to believe her. "I know what you want to confess. At least my father's version of the incident."

Gaping, he took a hasty step back.

"Now I want to hear your version." She prayed he wouldn't shut her out. Prayed he trusted her enough to listen and judge without bias. When he remained silent, she squeezed his hand. "Please, Jake."

"It was the summer before our senior year. I got off work early from the Quick-Lube and went home to change clothes. When I entered the house, I heard weird noises coming from my mom's bedroom."

He paused and Amanda insisted, "Go on."

"I thought maybe Mom had hit the bottle early and had gotten sick, so I walked right into the bedroom. Your dad was in bed with her."

Amanda closed her eyes and inwardly cringed at the image that flashed through her mind.

"I was shocked. Not that a guy was in bed with my mom, but that the man was a preacher. I left and waited on the porch. When your dad appeared, I expected him to apologize, repent or whatever the hell a preacher is supposed to do in that situation. Instead he gave the impression that his actions were permissible because my mother was white trash."

Amanda slapped a hand over her mouth and battled tears.

"When you offered to tutor me, I refused at first because you were the preacher's daughter. But then I realized I could use you to get back at your father. I'd planned to gain your trust, get you to like me, to have sex with you, then dump you as if you mattered little to me." He shrugged. "I'd intended to treat you the way your father treated my mother—with total disregard."

"But you didn't. Why?"

"Because you were kind, caring and sincere. Nothing like your old man. I couldn't hurt you, so I walked away."

"Oh, Jake." Amanda wanted to weep for the pain in his gaze.

"But in the end I was the one who paid the price for your father's actions."

"I don't understand."

He stroked her cheek, his gaze softening on her face. "I walked away from you in the physical sense. But you've always been with me here." He held her hand to his chest. "I never stopped loving you, Amanda."

She struggled against tears. "We've wasted so many years when we could have been together."

"But you shouldn't have to choose between me and your father."

"I've already chosen. And I choose you." She breathed deeply. "It will take time, but one day I hope to be able to forgive my father."

"For your sake, Amanda, I'll try to forgive him, too." He hugged her fiercely. "But no promises."

"The only promise I insist on is your love."

He sealed his promise with a kiss, then lifted her in his arms.

"I'm not helpless." Her protest sounded feeble to her own ears. What woman in her right mind wouldn't wish to be swept off her feet?

"You'll break your pretty neck in those sexy heels." He trudged up the rocky pathway. Instead of stopping at the boarded-up mine entrance, he carried her behind a large boulder, then set her on her feet near a smaller opening in the rock.

"There's a decent-size chamber inside that shoots off the main mine entrance."

"You want to go in there?"

Jake's breath brushed her mouth when he spoke. "I rode out here earlier today and got rid of all the creepy-crawly things. It's comfy and cozy inside."

Amanda's heart thumped crazily in her chest. So he hadn't planned on skipping town without her, as she'd feared. "You go first."

He slipped through the opening, then a moment later a shaft of light spilled from the secret hideaway. "Ready. Watch your head."

Carefully she edged inside. "Oh, my," she sighed, awed that Jake had turned the small cavern into a pleasure den. Aside from the lantern in the corner, he'd laid out thick blankets, and a bottle of red wine and two goblets stuck out of a picnic basket.

She sank to the blankets, her legs curled to the side. "So this is where all the high-school guys brought their girlfriends to make out."

"Not all the guys." Jake's face turned ruddy.

"You never made out with a girl here?"

He shook his head, his expression open and vulnerable. "You're my first."

He kissed her while his hands slipped her dress straps off her shoulder, his fingers leaving a trail of fire across her skin. Before the heat of his touch cooled, his mouth replaced his hands and Amanda found herself on her back, gazing up at Jake's face.

This is right. Perfect. Her mind and heart agreed—here and now with Jake was her destiny. Whatever the future held for them as a couple, Amanda would always cherish the memories of this hometown Fourth of July weekend.

Jake's kisses worked their magic as she gave herself over to the moment. Not until a cool breeze caressed her breasts did she realize that her dress bunched around her waist. Jake stared boldly at her body, his hands busy shoving the material over her hips and down her legs. Clad only in her panties and high heels, she reveled in the pleasure she read in his face as he perused her seminaked form. When his fingers joined his visual pursuit, Amanda arched her back seeking more—seeking Jake.

He lavished attention on her breasts, his tongue creating a glistening path across her skin. At the same time he slipped his hand beneath the waistband of her panties.

"I can't wait," he breathed into her mouth.

With a quickness that belied his size, he leaped from the blanket and stripped off his tux.

She soaked up the sight of his glorious nudity and thought she'd never viewed anything more beautiful than Jake's lean muscular physique. There was an aura of wildness about his aroused state, yet also a raw vulnerability in his eyes. With Jake it would never be *just sex*. It would always be *love*.

Amanda rose to her knees and ran her hands up his legs, the back of his thighs, his muscular buttocks. She wrapped her fingers around him and stroked, reveling in the groan that rumbled in his chest as his head dropped back and his eyes closed. She rubbed her mouth against his navel, then swirled her tongue inside. A moment later Jake sprawled atop her.

"These are coming off." He tugged her panties down her thighs. The elastic band caught on her heel. She reached to remove her shoe, but he grabbed her knee and instructed, "Leave them on."

Feeling a little naughty, she grinned. "Whatever you wish."

Their hands and mouths engaged in a game of who could arouse whom more. At the touch of Jake's lips on the inside of her thigh, Amanda raised a mental white flag. Jake ignored her surrender, his fingers serenading her aroused flesh. Her heart pounded, her pulse raced. Her reach for release became painful in its intensity. Then Jake's mouth replaced his hand and she soared through the heavens, uncaring that her cries echoed down the mountainside.

Amanda hadn't caught her breath before Jake sheathed himself and slid inside her. Her muscles, still convulsing from her climax, squeezed him. Stroke after stroke, he dragged her back up the mountainside.

She wrapped her legs around his waist, her high heels digging into his hips. His thrusts became frenzied, and Amanda grasped his head and tugged his face near. When he sought her mouth, she held him off with a hand in the center of his chest. "I love you." Threading her fingers through his damp hair, she kissed him with all the love and desire she'd held inside for so long.

"You're all I've ever wanted, needed, to be happy, Amanda."

Jake's lovemaking intensified, and before she'd even recovered from her first climax, she tumbled off the rocky hillside again. Jake followed, grunting his release against her neck.

Save for their labored breathing, they lay in the stillness, their slippery bodies entwined. Jake buried his face in Amanda's neck, battling the lump forming in his throat. Making love with her had been a gut-wrenching experience. He'd expected their lovemaking to be special, but he hadn't been prepared to connect with her on such a deep level. After his screwed-up childhood he'd believed his heart was impenetrable. Damned if Amanda hadn't blown right through the organ.

In her arms Jake felt as if he mattered. As if Amanda couldn't live without his touch, his kiss, his loving. Somehow, she'd made him believe he was her everything.

Lifting his head, he studied her blue eyes. "I've never loved anyone before. Never even came close. But I swear, Amanda, I'm head over heels for you."

"I love you just as much."

Face sober, he tucked her against his side. "Then we've got a problem, Winslow."

"We do?"

"Your life is here in Silver Cliff and mine's in California." His chest expanded with a deep breath. "I thought I could, but I'm not ready to move back here. The memories are too…" He swallowed hard. "But if it's where you want to live…"

She trailed her fingers across the muscled ridges of his stomach. "We deserve a fresh start."

"But your friends are in Silver Cliff. Your home. Your job," he argued.

"Jake, are you asking me to marry you or just be with you?"

Hell, he was making a mess of things. "To marry me, of course…unless you'd rather—"

"Yes, Jake, I'll marry you."

Emotion throbbed in his chest. "I don't know what I did to deserve your love," he confessed. "I can give you a good life. A big house. A fancy car."

"I don't want material things, Jake." She caressed his chest. "This…your heart…your love is all I need."

"Then it's yours, babe."

"Good. Now that we've settled that, I will admit the whole white knight rescuing me from the small mountain town holds some appeal."

He chuckled, amazed this beautiful woman with such a generous, warm heart was forever his.

"Take me to places I've only read about in library books. Then when we're old and tired and we've seen the world, we'll return to Silver Cliff and spend the rest of our days meddling in everyone's business and generally creating an uproar riding your Harley around town."

"What about kids?" He wasn't sure what kind of father he'd make, but he trusted Amanda to show him the way.

"A couple of babies would add to the adventure." She curled a hand around his neck. "Since my biological clock is ticking rather loudly these days, we'd better begin our little family right away."

Because Jake was through running, he was more than happy to oblige. "Whatever you say, babe."

A BABY ON THE WAY
Laura Marie Altom

Dear Reader,

Even though I've always been a "good girl" and married a "good boy," there's a mischievous part of me that still wonders about the "bad boys" of the world. What makes them tick? What happens when those boys grow into men? Are they still naughty, or do they change their rebellious ways?

This story was a hoot to write, because in dreaming up hunky Graydon, I got to vicariously see not only what a true "bad boy" was like, but how a "good girl" like India might handle taming him. Turns out that just as for the scary punk rocker I landed as my freshman college roommate, appearances—or, in Graydon's case, perceptions—can be deceiving!

I hope you'll enjoy India's exploration of Graydon as much as I enjoyed writing it.

Laura Marie

For her generous donation
to the northeast Oklahoma chapter of
ASHRAE, Mary Bowers won dedication rights to this
story. When I asked how she wanted her dedication
phrased, this is what she said:

"I would like to dedicate this book
to my four grandchildren, Ryan, Daniel,
Addy and Laura. You are the lights of my life and
I am so proud of you for your accomplishments.
Since you are all such good students and love
to read, I am dedicating this to you. Love, Mimi."

Beautifully put, Mary.
Thanks again for your generous spirit!

Chapter One

Welcome, Silver Cliff Eagles!

India Foster glanced at the banner stretched across the Silver Palace Hotel's teeming lobby, then groaned. Talk about leaping from the frying pan into the fire…

After the solitude of her two-day drive from Columbus, Ohio, to Silver Cliff—a small, Colorado mountain town—finding herself drowning in a crowd felt surreal. Still, as the hotel's newly-hired conference and event coordinator, India knew wrangling mobs like this was a large part of her job. She just hadn't expected to do it quite so soon. And wouldn't have, if not for her sister, Lyndsay, flaking out on her.

Upon India's arrival at the apartment they'd planned to share, the building manager had handed her a note: Off to L.A. Long story. Happy B-Day!

Right. Too bad birthdays couldn't be postponed.

Better yet, in India's case, canceled altogether.

The potbellied guy had further brightened her day by explaining that the entire county had been invaded by Silver Cliff High graduates, in town for a reunion to both celebrate and mourn the end of an era. The old high school was being converted into luxury condos. Apparently, the new school was state-of-the-art, but many older graduates were taking the closing hard. Having herself gone to high school in Pershing,

Ohio, Class of 2000, she'd been more choked up about not having a place to stay than by the closing of Silver Cliff High.

Because it was the Fourth of July, any nearby hotels and motels not overwhelmed with graduates were booked with tourists. She'd hoped to find a temporary home here at the Silver Palace, but now that she'd planted herself and her rock-heavy overnight bag at the end of a long line crawling to the front desk, she knew from the pit in her stomach that she might end up sleeping in her car.

"Pardon." Someone tapped India's shoulder.

"Yes?" India turned to face a middle-aged woman wearing a disastrous red-and-black striped dress. She carried a clip-board in the crook of one arm. In the other arm, a basket threatened to overflow with numbered pins.

"Didn't you read a word of your registration packet? You can't get in *this* line without first visiting mine." As if she were a teacher scolding an unruly child, the woman shook her head and clucked her tongue. "Jill Benson, I thought I'd taught you better than that. Always, always read and follow directions."

"Sorry, but you must have me mistaken for—"

"Here you go," the woman said, snatching an '04 button from her basket, then fastening it to India's pink chambray shirt. "Can't have you running around naked, so to speak."

"But I'm not—"

"Tommy Underwood, if I've told you once I've…"

Before India got a word in edgewise, the woman was off, accosting another victim. India started to remove the button, then figured there was no point. She'd probably just get nailed anew. This way, she'd at least blend with the crowd.

Shifting her overnight bag from one hand to the other, she moved up in line, vowing that her sister would pay for putting her through this.

Scowling, India decided that out of a record number of awful birthdays, this one was the last straw. No cake, no presents, no breaking out in song she could handle, but this crushing sense of yet again being alone in a crowd hurt.

Which was why she'd moved halfway across the country. To finally fill the gnawing hunger stemming from never belonging. In the two years Lyndsay had lived in Silver Cliff, she'd characterized the town as sweet and as welcoming as a scoop of hot-fudge-drenched ice cream, and had repeatedly urged India to pack up and move in with her. Lyndsay being Lyndsay, though, she hadn't put much stock in India actually finishing her degree. However, now that India was armed with her diploma and had this amazing new job, she felt certain only good things were to come. Surely fate wouldn't be so cruel as to put her through the stress of the past couple of months only to land her in fresh trouble.

Steeling her shoulders, raising her chin and inching farther up in line, India vowed not to think of this latest development as trouble but an adventure.

Thirty minutes later, at last taking her turn at the sumptuous hotel's ivory-toned marble registration counter, that adventure India had convinced herself she was seeking was firmly back to being trouble!

"But I'm supposed to start work Monday," India said to the front manager, whose name tag read *Vicki.* "I've already tried every other conceivable place in town. Please, I'll sleep in my new office. I really need a place to stay."

"I understand," Vicki said warmly. "Your new boss is one of my dearest friends, and if it wasn't for my husband's sister and what feels like her fourteen kids staying with me, I'd offer you *my* guest room, but—"

"I don't mean to interrupt," said a grinning brunette who'd been complaining to a clerk about one of her roommates having canceled, and therefore no longer sharing the bill. Unless she was a fellow impostor graduate, she was, as her button proudly proclaimed, a graduate of the Class of '02.

"But seeing as how my sisters and I just lost a roommate and you need a room, would you consider staying with us?"

HER HOUSING CRISIS temporarily resolved thanks to the incredibly kind set of triplets, with whom she'd become fast friends, India was grateful that at least some of her birthday angst had been assuaged. She figured that now her best course of action would be to launch an apartment hunt.

Trouble was, she was starving and in need of a bathroom.

Given that the lobby still thronged with graduates, India decided to fill both needs elsewhere. She hefted her overnight bag to the triplets' room, then charted a course through the human sea for the hotel's revolving brass door.

She'd almost reached freedom when a funny thing happened. She sidestepped two rowdy boys, only to be stunned by a guy. Not just *any* guy, but the kind of chiseled, fully grown movie-star perfection she'd bought in poster form as a teen, then used to decorate her bedroom. He seemed equally determined to barrel right through the throng. Only, not to the nearest exit—but to her!

Still at a polite distance, he said, "If you've ever been hurt by a member of the opposite sex, then I hope you'll forgive me."

"For what?"

He grinned, then hauled off and kissed her.

Kissed her!

Wonderfully, wickedly kissed her till she was weak-kneed and dizzy and rethinking her earlier plan to cancel her birthday. How could she, when this bad-boy stranger with spiky dark hair, a hint of stubble and a rock-hard, six-foot body encased in faded jeans and a black Burton Snowboard T-shirt had just bestowed on her a dizzying gift.

"Sorry," the guy said over a recently set up string quartet and still more chattering graduates. "Emergency."

Hands to flaming cheeks, willing her pulse to slow, India stammered, "E-emergency kissing?"

"Hey, what can I say?" Stepping closer to avoid being trampled by three blue-haired women wearing oversize Class of '43 buttons on their lapels, he graced her with a white-toothed grin as sinfully sexy as his kiss. "You're hot, and that woman over there?" He pointed across the crowd. "The tall brunette on the hulk's arm? She's *not*. Hot, that is."

"She looks pretty to me." The woman wearing a '96 badge that matched the kissing bandit's had inky hair and a porcelain complexion that gave her an exotic appearance. Her black linen pantsuit fit like a dream and her matching purse and shoes looked as though they'd cost more than a month of India's salary. The muscled Nordic guy with her also wore black, but as a man's suit. "He's not bad, either—assuming you go for Neanderthal."

"Bite your tongue. The guy's a germ."

"Steal your girl?"

"In a manner of speaking."

"So then far from you kissing me because of love at first sight, you just wanted her to see you having a great time with a younger woman?"

"Damn." He reddened, ducked his head. "Here I don't even know your name, and already you see right through me."

She smiled and thrust out her hand. "India Foster, full-time event planner, part-time love doctor."

The ruggedly handsome stranger fit his palm to hers, shocking her with tingly awareness. Was it normal for her to crave another kiss after knowing the guy barely two minutes? "Graydon Johnson, snowboard coach and person very much in need of your services."

India couldn't help but laugh at his antics, although the pain lurking just beneath the surface of his slow, sexy grin was palpable.

"Class of 2004, huh?" He nodded at the big button the overzealous organizer had pinned on her chest. "You *are* a young thing."

"Actually—"

"Graydon."

That brunette who'd been pretty from across the room? Up close and personal—as in Graydon's face—she was ravishing.

"I'd hoped to bump into you. Did Jake take his allergy medicine to camp?"

"Yes."

"Wonderful. You know how I worry." Hulk in tow, she sashayed off with a polished squeal to greet a fellow brunette.

"Grrr…" Graydon shook his head, eyeing his ex. "That woman couldn't melt ice cubes on her—"

"Graydon!" A trio of grinning women in red-, silver-and-black cheerleader uniforms, wearing '94 buttons, bounced and jiggled their way over. India had doubts whether the seams of the decade-old uniform of the freckle-faced redhead would hold. After a round of hugs and small talk, during which India gleaned that the man who'd kissed her wasn't merely a coach but a recently retired professional snowboarder who now managed both pros and future Olympians, she was starting to feel very much out of her league.

Having been born on the wrong side of the tracks to a flower-child mother who'd vanished with the wind one day when India was four and her sister two, India had never felt part of the school establishment. While other kids had had moms and dads who'd volunteered, India's dad had sometimes had a job and most of the time was a drunk.

That she'd worked her way through college was one of India's proudest achievements. It had taken six years, but she'd done it. And now, bright and early Monday morning, she'd begin a new phase of her life as the Sliver Palace conference and event coordinator. With her hotel-management degree and promising future, India knew in her head she had nothing to feel inferior about. The past was gone.

She raised her chin, fighting the knot in her throat, forcing a smile. Whether her sister cared to join her or not, damn it, she was officially launching a new life, and old ghosts weren't welcome.

"Good Lord," Graydon said, words warm in her left ear once the cheerleaders had giggled their way to someone new. "I've gotta get out of here. How about I buy you a drink?"

"I, um, don't. Drink, that is."

"O-okay. Do you eat?"

Laughing, India replied, "That is a skill at which I'm most adept."

"Excellent," he said with a broad smile. "It appears we have something in common—besides, of course, having graduated from the same high school and kissing."

"Yes, well—"

"Graydon!" A twenty-something, long-haired guy with glasses and a neon-pink T-shirt wandered up to shake Graydon's hand. Four more men in equally obnoxious clothes followed.

India had been about to explain how she wasn't a fellow Silver Cliff graduate, when she found herself yet again cut off at the proverbial pass. Still hungry and now needing a ladies' room in the worst way, she waved at her new friend, then said, "Looks like you're busy. I'm going to go."

Cutting off one of the guys, he asked, "Will you be at this afternoon's picnic or tonight's fireworks?"

"Depends," she said, truly unsure if she'd have the time or energy. "If I do make it, maybe I'll see you there."

"Yeah. Maybe." Their gazes locked, and then, as abruptly as he'd entered her life, Graydon Johnson was gone.

Chapter Two

What had he been thinking?

Strolling along Boulder Avenue, surrounded by historic brick storefronts bedecked in red, white and blue bunting and American flags, Graydon Johnson tuned out the ramblings of his old pals Chuck, Ted and Phillip who'd talked him into attending the reunion, to instead focus on her. India Foster. Or, more specifically, why in the hell he had regressed to pulling such a juvenile stunt.

If he'd had his way, she'd be here with him, giving him a chance to apologize again. Part of the reason he'd returned to Silver Cliff was to prove to not just the world but himself that he'd changed. But that kiss had been a move straight out of his past. He'd been temporarily insane, needing to show Tiff he'd moved on. Apparently, he hadn't *moved* as far as he'd hoped in the right direction.

So why had he kissed a complete stranger?

Pride. To prove to his ex-wife that even though she didn't find him desirable, other women did.

Um, question, his conscience interjected. *How do you know India wanted you, when you didn't give her a choice?*

Jaw hardened, Graydon vowed to put the incident behind him. The long weekend was about making a fresh start, claiming second chances. Sure, he might bump into India

Foster here and there, but it wouldn't mean anything. She'd no doubt already forgotten the whole incident. The way he needed to.

In the two years since retiring as a professional snowboarder and finalizing his and Tiffany's divorce, then single-handedly raising their son, Graydon was proud to have finally become a man. Trouble was, no one outside the circle of folks he worked with daily seemed to take his newfound maturity seriously. It was as if everyone he'd known back in high school and on the pro circuit had frozen him in time.

"This okay?" Phillip asked, stopping in front of one of Graydon's favorite haunts. Big Air was the kind of bar he used to hang out in after competitions. Smoky. Rowdy. Underground indie rock pulsing so fast it changed the pace of his heart. On a Thursday afternoon, the place wasn't quite so wild, yet all it took was a glance to know that going inside led down a potentially dangerous road.

"What's wrong?" Chuck asked, holding open the door. Metallica blared over the jukebox, bringing on an instant headache.

"Sorry, guys," Graydon said, hand clamped around Chuck's shoulder, "but I just thought of something I have to do."

"What's more important than hanging with us?" Phillip complained.

Calling my son.

"SURE YOU DON'T WANT me to stick around and help with that?" Still full from the delicious lunch she'd downed in a tucked-away Chinese place, India gestured at the mountain of paperwork threatening to avalanche from Emily Richards's, her new boss's, desk.

"Nah," Emily said with a breezy laugh—one of about a gazillion factors leading India to take the job. Not only did the position as event coordinator pay well, but it would be fun and involve working with great people like Emily. Best of all, it would be a huge first step in fulfilling her most cherished dream of finally finding a home. Not just a place to live, but a real *home.*

The one dark cloud had been Lyndsay's abrupt exit. But that was okay. Just as India needed roots, Lyndsay had always needed to fly. If unable to share physical closeness, she and her sister would have to settle for a less tangible, though equally fulfilling, spiritual relationship.

"Really," Emily said, backlit by the golden setting sun and a spectacular alpine view. "It's your birthday. I'm sorry your initial apartment search was a bust, but I'll ask around here and see what we can turn up. In the meantime, go on ahead to the fireworks with your new roommates. I'll soon be fetching my kids and hubby, then heading that way."

"Sure?"

Again laughing, this time adding a wink, Emily said, "Girl, seeing as how you're not even supposed to start till Monday, you're gonna have to curb this enthusiasm. Otherwise the general manager will be giving you my job!"

"BET TWENTY BUCKS you can't jump off the roof of that picnic pavilion, then do a full rotation before landing feetfirst in the trash can." The worst part about Phillip's nutty dare was the sincerity accompanying his go-for-it expression.

"Listen," Graydon said from his perch on top of a concrete picnic table at Canyon Lake State Park, "we're pushing thirty. What about that fact do you not get?"

"What I do get," Phillip said, shaking his head, then pitching an empty beer can onto a patch of grass, "is that you've lost it, man. We all thought that once you wrenched free of Tiffany's evil clutches, you'd be back. But—"

"Look." Graydon pushed to his feet, nodding at not just Phillip but Chuck and Ted. "Unlike you bozos, I've got responsibilities. As for Tiff's leaving, I had no choice in the matter.

Her splitting was a wake-up call. We're not getting any younger. Do you seriously want to still be hanging out with our boards, doling out dares, when we're, like, fifty?"

"Hell yeah," Phillip said. "Either that or dead."

For that asinine comment, Graydon gave the guy's shoulder a slug.

"Ouch. What was that for?"

"Being a tool. Grow up, man."

"Yeah, sure," Phillip complained. "I'll grow up when you wise up and drop this reformed act. Everybody knows you're a wild child, Gray. Are you trying to act all upright and respectable for Tiff? You know, trying to get her back? Well, news flash. You've got the eye of the tiger in you, and just because you declare that beast tamed doesn't make it so. You're only twenty-eight. For you to be retired is bogus. A waste of God-given talent."

Graydon snorted, then knelt to pick up his so-called friend's litter. "Catch you later. I'm off to find adult conversation."

"Off to find an early grave!" Phillip shouted.

Graydon fought the urge to flip him a backhanded bird.

"SO THEN WHAT?" India asked the triplets and their classmates in regards to their outrageous tale of having duped some poor day skier up from Colorado Springs into dating three of them on the same night.

"What do you think?" Carly said, a twinkle in her eye. "He fell madly in love with me, and I still see him occasionally."

"No, you don't." Carly's sister Callie frowned. "I saw him just last week."

"Get out," their third sister, Cammie, said. "I've got a date with him next week."

Grinning, shaking her head along with the rest of the crowd, India said, "Looks to me, ladies, like this guy had the last laugh." Pushing to her feet from the boulder she'd perched on,

India aimed for the log-cabin bathrooms about a hundred yards down a pine-needle-strewn trail.

The night was crisp and clear. With the temperature in the low fifties, her scarlet-and-gray Ohio State hoodie was a welcome, if not fashion-forward, touch to her outfit of faded jeans, sneakers and the Rocky Mountain High T-shirt she'd picked up at the Dillon outlet mall in her previous day's travels.

Soaring pines and Douglas firs scented the air, invigorating her steps. Laughing children twirled sparklers. A ragtime band played patriotic favorites. Red, white and blue bunting, streamers and flags completed the park's holiday perfection, validating her decision to make this idyllic place home.

India had finished in the bathroom—an increasingly familiar hangout—and was on her way back to her new friends, when she stopped to tie her left shoe.

Bam!

One second she'd been crouching; the next she'd toppled onto her side on a pillow of pine needles, more shocked than hurt.

"India," Graydon said, kneeling alongside her. He brushed needles from her shoulders and combed them from her hair. His touch was so tender, so unexpected and warm and oddly familiar in this lakeside forest park thick with strangers, that she couldn't help but grin. "I'm so sorry. You all right?"

"Geez, Graydon," she teased. "If you wanted to see me again, you could've just asked."

"I know." He helped her back onto her feet. "But I've never been one to take the easy route. Again, I'm sorry."

"It's okay," she said, lingering in his arms probably longer than necessary but not caring. It was her birthday, and he was a gorgeous hunk of man. Kind, gentle and sweet. Tomorrow she had a hundred things to do—finding an apartment, unloading her car, grocery shopping, starting utilities. Just thinking about it was exhausting. Here, now, all she wanted was more fun.

"Seriously, do you need a doctor?"

"Graydon—" she shook her head, clinging to his muscular forearms "—I'm fine. The pine needles broke my fall—which wasn't far to begin with."

"Okay, well…" They stood there for a few seconds, the world—rather, *his* world—bustling around them. Would she attend her own ten-year high-school reunion? Probably not. What was the point? It wasn't as if anyone would even remember her name. She'd changed schools so many times that she'd learned to be invisible. Moving among the other kids like a ghost; attending classes and making good grades, but never truly belonging, as Graydon clearly did, judging by the friendly nods he received from the guys and the adoring stares from the passing women. All of which reminded her no matter how much she was enjoying the moment, good things eventually came to an end.

Graydon, unlike her ex, Zack, definitely fell under the heading *good!*

"See that bench over there?" He pointed to a hand-hewn log seat for two alongside the glassy lake.

"Uh-huh."

"See those sticky-faced kids making a beeline for it?"

"Uh-huh…"

Lacing his fingers with hers, he gave her a tug. "Let's beat 'em."

Laughing, she ran for all she was worth to keep up with Graydon's long-legged stride, and they did beat the children. The two boys and four girls didn't seem too broken up about it, though. They settled at the foot of a stubby dock that allowed for plenty of opportunity to dunk everything from rocks to twigs to pinecones into the still water.

"You're pretty fast," Graydon said, not the least winded.

"You're supersonic," India complained, resting her elbows on her knees, fighting for oxygen in the thin mountain air. "You must still live around here to be used to the altitude."

"Nah. I'm now based in Lake Placid. My folks moved there last year to be closer to Jake, so aside from when I'm touring with the team, I stick to one to three thousand feet."

"Not to be nosy, but who's Jake?"

"Sorry. He's my seven-year-old son." Ever the proud pop, Graydon whipped out his wallet and the plastic-sheathed photos he kept on hand. "Here he is at his first half-pipe competition, and this is one of him just before last summer's Skate Fest. He backed out at the last minute. I told him to not let it get him down. You know, some days you just aren't ready. He's a great kid. Means the world to me—as opposed to…"

"The woman you were trying to wow earlier with your kissing prowess?"

"Ouch." He winced. "Guess I had that coming. Yes, she would be Tiffany, my ex-wife."

"So then you have custody?"

"Yep."

"If you don't mind my asking, what happened? Between you and your wife."

"Short version—one day I got back from a competition circuit to find her waiting at the front door, bags packed. She said she was tired of me never being home, of her always being alone with Jake."

"So her answer to addressing those issues was to leave home?"

"Pretty much."

India whistled. "I understand why emotionally you'd still be rough around the edges."

"Tell me about it," Graydon said with a sad shake of his head.

"Speaking of, ah, rocky former significant others…the guy I was hooked up with left the morning I told him I was pregnant with his child."

"No-o-o-o."

"Yes."

"How far along are you?"

"Six weeks, so the whole scorned-lover thing is kinda new, but with hormones raging and all, I'm catching on fast."

Pregnant.

Wow. He hadn't seen that coming.

As the night wore on, Graydon tried wiping that fact from his mind, but for him the knowledge was the room's big pink elephant…the slap in the face he'd needed to remind himself why he'd come to this reunion: to once and for all prove to his old crowd that he was a changed man.

Nice speech, but where did that leave him in regard to his ever-growing fascination with India's smile?

Chapter Three

A short while later, during a conversational lull, India revisited a topic she and Graydon had skipped over earlier. "So you live in Lake Placid, huh? As in New York?"

"Ever been?"

Ha! "This is my first trip outside of Ohio." But thanks to her dad, she had lived in what had felt like darn near every city in the state.

"How can that be if this is your hometown? I mean, you did graduate from Silver Cliff High, right?"

"Um..." Nibbling the inside of her lower lip, India said, "I tried clearing that up earlier, but Tiffany got in the way. I didn't exactly go to your school—or even graduate in 2004. Just got adopted by that pushy lady with the buttons. I wanted to explain, but she—"

"Trust me," he said with a laugh, "you aren't the first to be steamrolled by Miss Blanchard."

After discussing her true high-school stats, he asked, "So? What brought you to town?"

India told him about Lyndsay having sung Silver Cliff's praises enough to make her yearn for a slice of the mountain heaven. "I thought that with my sister here, there could be no better place to raise my baby."

"What made your sister take off?"

"Don't have a clue. I keep getting the voice-mail message on her cell."

"Are you worried?"

"Not really. Of the two of us, Lyndsay's always been more of a free spirit. I'm the homebody type." Or, at least had wanted to be.

"She stay in touch with your folks?"

"Mom's been gone for twenty years."

"Like, dead?" He winced.

"Just gone." After picking up a twig at her feet, India snipped it into quarter-inch sections, thrilled for the distraction.

"Bet that must've been rough."

"In the beginning, but she was never really there in the first place, if you get my meaning."

"Unfortunately, I do," he said, hunching over and resting his elbows on his knees. "Reminds me of how I was as a father when Jake was born. Back then, I was pretty deep into the whole pro-circuit scene. Compete by day, party by night, travel so much in between that I'd wake not knowing where I was."

She glanced his way. "That's a heavy admission for a first date."

"That what this is?" he asked, tucking a small pine bough behind her ear. "A date?"

Mouth dry, pulse racing, inordinately aware of him beside her—not just physically, but of his vulnerability and depth of spirit—she shrugged, making an effort to play it cool. At the end of the reunion, he'd be heading back to New York. She'd just landed a dream job in a dreamy town. It didn't matter that with every fiber of her being, she ached to somehow soothe the sadness behind Graydon's half smile. She had her own emotional wounds to heal. So, knowing all that, why couldn't she stop herself from asking, "Would you want it to be? A date?"

In fading twilight, his gaze locking with hers in a dark-eyed stare so intense she almost stopped breathing, he nodded, then shook his head. Chuckling, he said, "I don't know what I want, other than to sit here on this bench and spend the rest of the night watching fireworks with you."

"And later? When the fireworks are over?"

He leaned in for a long, lingering, thoroughly enjoyable kiss. Softly, sweetly, he stroked her tongue, muddling her mind with heat and urges and needs she'd thought forever gone along with her lousy ex. Graydon tasted faintly of beer and watermelon and man—all man.

Turning to him in the darkness, easing her arms around his neck, sliding her fingers into his hair, India ignored the alarms ringing in her head. As a soon-to-be mom, she had no business making out on a very public park bench with a man she hardly knew. It didn't matter that she felt as if she'd always known him. What mattered was providing a safe, secure home for her baby. A home in which all tension was removed, leaving only peace.

But then the evening's show started with a glorious explosion of fireworks, mimicking the tiny explosions in her chest.

Why did her freshly wounded heart insist on galloping every time she met Graydon's heated gaze? Shouldn't she still be cautious after what had happened with Zack? Why, with everything in her, did she want to stay on this bench, Graydon beside her, till the crowd thinned, and longer still till the sun rose?

"Darlin'," her "date" said, coming up for air, his handsome face reflecting the sky's dazzling color, "as for what happens after the fireworks…I've got a sinking suspicion that where the two of us are concerned, they may never end."

Knowing he was right, yet accepting the impossibility of their ever sharing much more than this one shining moment, India's mood turned melancholy.

GRAYDON KISSED HER again, slowly, deeply, hoping to rock India's soul as blasts rocked the ground at their feet. Something about the woman made him crazy. Kissing her was akin to snowboarding fresh powder faster than he knew was safe, but the high of her kisses stole all reason. Odds were, with the dozens of activities the reunion committee had planned, he wouldn't get the chance to see this beauty again. Of course, he shouldn't *want* to see India again. But something about her made the bad boy still in him stand up and roar.

Drawing back, he cupped her cheeks, his gaze locked with hers. At the unexpected sadness in her eyes, he asked, "Everything all right?"

She nodded.

"Then what's with the pouty look?"

"I don't pout."

"News flash," he teased, "you are now."

She sighed, gently pushed him away. "We shouldn't be doing this."

"Talking?" His failed attempt to be serious had her shooting him a glare.

"You know what I mean. I'm about to be a parent. I'm setting down roots. I can't just run around town kissing the first boy I meet."

"Yeah," he said, agreeing with her in that he, too, had no business indulging in a fling. "But I'm all man."

"Stop," she said, laughing while nudging him to the other side of the bench. "I mean it."

"I know."

"And?" she urged.

"And…as much as it sickens my male pride to admit it, you're right." *But that's as far as I'm willing to go. I'm not willing to apologize again for kissing you, when your lips are the best thing to happen to me in months. Hell—years!* "Tonight should be the end of the road for us."

"I agree. I've got a ton of stuff to do tomorrow."

"Me, too."

"So where does that leave us?"

Feeling all of ten, he reached for her hands, eased his fingers between hers, brushing her palms with the pads of his thumbs. A knot in the pit of his stomach had him damn near as low as the day he'd announced his early pro retirement from the sport he loved.

"Graydon?"

He glanced up, to discover—unfortunately—that night's shadows had made India prettier, more intriguing, than ever. A few runaway curls escaped her messy ponytail, giving him the asinine urge to capture one and use it to tug her to him for another kiss. Mouth dry, he somehow managed to swallow. "Yeah?"

"What do you want to do?"

He kissed her again.

A full, delicious minute later, she said, "That wasn't exactly what I'd had in mind as an answer."

"Complaining?"

"No, but…"

"I know." Back to cupping her cheeks, he rested his forehead against hers and sighed. "In answer to your question where does all this leave us? While it's depressing to admit, I'm afraid that after tonight, the two of us will probably just be a great memory."

"YOUR ROOMIES TOLD ME I'd find you here."

"Hey." Friday morning, India glanced up from the newspaper's apartment classifieds to find Graydon not in her mind's eye but strolling through the door of the hotel employee's lounge in all his handsome glory. Like every other place in the grand old hotel, the lounge was elegant, done in rich cream, with striking silver and jewel-toned accents. Hotel management believed that if employees felt special, their contentment would trickle down to the guests. So far, from everyone India had met, the theory proved out. Though she didn't officially start her new career till Monday, already she felt at home among her future coworkers. The one place she didn't feel quite at ease was in Graydon's commanding presence. His piercing gaze caused her pulse to race. "Thought you were off hiking with your old pals."

He shrugged, helping himself to the lounge chair beside hers. "I was, but…"

"But what?" His open-ended statement left her folding her newspaper with the circled ads facing out. It looked as though her apartment hunt was momentarily on hold.

"I don't know." He shook his head. "All that my buddies want to do is thrill-seeking stuff I have no business participating in."

"What kind of stuff?"

"For starters, bungee jumping off Dead Man's Gorge."

"Mmm… Sounds like fun." She winced.

He chuckled. "To be straight with you, it is."

"Then how come you're not up there taking the plunge?"

Sighing, he said, "I'm a dad. A professional. I have responsibilities not only to my son but to the boarders I coach. What if I got hurt? Who'd care for Jake? Who'd see my guys through their competitive seasons?"

"Well—" India angled in the overstuffed chair to face him "—in an emergency, your fellow coaches could take over your protégées and Tiffany could step in with Jake, don't you think?"

Graydon snorted. "She already left him once. Who says she wouldn't again? Besides which, supposedly, a big part of the reason she left me was because of my 'wild, thrill-seeking ways.' I don't want to be like that anymore. Not just because it's time I grew up, but so that Jake has a father he can rely on."

With a considering nod, India digested what Graydon had just admitted. What kind of woman was Tiffany to have left him when he was apparently trying hard to overcome past sins? But then, not knowing the other woman's side, maybe it was Tiffany's drastic step that had jolted Graydon onto a straight-and-narrow path? For all India knew, part of his driving force to now be superdad could be to impress Tiffany into taking him back.

Mouth dry at the idea that the special moments they'd shared may have been little more than rebound kisses, India tucked her hair behind her ears. After swigging from the bottled water she'd found in the lounge fridge, she asked, "So then earlier—you know, when Tiffany thought you weren't fit husband material—you feel you also let Jake down?"

"Yes. Maybe. I don't know." Tracing the upholstery's swirling cream-on-cream pattern, he added, "How do you judge intangibles like that? I mean, since his birth, the little guy's meant the world to me. His mother used to. Once Jake was walking and talking, I cut way back on my touring schedule—hell, cut my partying, too—but it was never enough, so I quit the pro tour altogether. Even that wasn't sufficient."

"Not that it's any of my business, but did you ever think nothing would've been? Good enough, that is? Maybe while you were out on the road, earning a living for your family, Tiffany changed. For that matter, maybe you never knew her at all. That's how it was for me with Zack."

"Yeah, but you were only with him a few weeks. I was with Tiff years."

"True." Meaning what? That just because India's time with her ex had been brief, albeit intense, it hadn't mattered? That her pain wasn't valid?

Sulking, India grabbed for her paper.

Apparently, the kind, compassionate man she'd been with the night before had been just a dream, because at the moment, she felt stung by the realities of the harsh light of day.

"I'm sorry," she said, "about whatever happened with your

wife, but even though Zack and I were together only a short while, trust me, I'm hurting, too. I may not be heartbroken, but I'm carrying his child, which comes with its own set of troubles. Like you, whether I like it or not, I'll share a lifelong connection to an ex that I'd give anything to sever. Not that I don't want this baby. Just that I wish he or she had been conceived under happier, more stable, circumstances."

"Hey…"

Graydon's voice had softened. He eased his fingers between hers. His touch felt indescribably natural. As if it wasn't a place called home she'd been seeking, but a person. As if wherever this stranger who'd burst into her life would be, was also where she'd find safety and shelter and strength. All of which was ludicrous, considering she hadn't yet known him twenty-four hours!

"Sorry," he said. "That came out wrong. I in no way meant to imply that what you're going through isn't rough. And to prove it, how about letting me take you to breakfast?"

"Thanks," she said, ire melting at his words, "but I already ate." *Besides which, as much as Tiffany apparently found you unpalatable, I could eat you up.* And that, too, made no sense, given that in a few days he'd return to Lake Placid and she'd launch into her new life. As she knew only too well from her time with Zack, hot guys came and went, but opportunities like the one she'd been gifted with at the Silver Palace didn't happen along every day.

"In that case," Graydon said, snatching up her newspaper from where she'd placed it on the coffee table, "how about I show off my vast local knowledge by helping you find a great place to stay?"

India knew that as attracted to Graydon as she was, her best course would be flying solo on the apartment-hunting mission, but the prospect of spending more time with him was appealing. As a bonus, she'd get more done with him than without.

After all, who better to have as her own personal guide than a man who'd grown up in the place she and her baby would from now on be living in?

"Well?" he asked, giving her shoulder a nudge. "I know some great, out-of-the-way places reserved for locals only. One word from me and doors will magically open."

At his earnest expression, she laughed. "Think that highly of yourself, do you?"

Chapter Four

"Is it someone's turn to apologize?" Graydon inquired, words nearly lost in the winding stream's gurgle. As promised, he'd followed through in hooking up India with a great place to live. His mom's old canasta buddy, Margaret Walters, was as sentimental as ever about leasing her furnished guesthouse—a pint-size, fairy-tale chalet tucked in a towering pine forest—to friends only. Her long-deceased husband had built the place, hoping to encourage their children and grandchildren to visit more often. Too bad for them that when they came now, there were so many that Margaret put them up at the Silver Palace. Meaning, India had just gotten lucky.

"There's no way Margaret's willing to rent something like this for so little. As adorable as it is, she could easily get double what she's asking."

"True, but as she pointed out," he said with a happy jingle of the keys, "it's never been her practice to price-gouge a friend."

"But I'm not her friend. She doesn't know me from Adam."

"Ever heard of a friend by association?"

"Sure, but—"

"Face it," he said, drawing her into his arms for a hug, resting his chin atop her head, breathing in her clean, soapy smell, "you've now entered the twilight zone of small-town life. All hope of privacy has been lost, but you gain friendships that'll last your whole life long." Releasing her not because he wanted to but because, in the very act of her signing a year-long lease with Margaret, India had also signed away any and all hope of exploring their relationship further, Graydon fought a flash of frustration. "Simply by knowing me, you now know everyone I do." He snorted. "A fact that could be good or bad."

Shaking her head and grinning, she released a good-natured groan, then mounted the steps to a deck overhanging the tumbling stream. She rested her elbows on the wooden railing, her expression serene. "You can't imagine what a dream come true this is for me," she said. "I grew up in seedy apartments that reeked of cooked cabbage and cheap cologne. To now have this…" She straightened, shifted her hands protectively over her stomach.

Never had Graydon seen a woman look more beautiful. Never had he wanted to kiss a woman more. Never had he been more acutely aware of his vow to become a changed man.

India was clearly getting her life on track. Everything was coming together for her. Job, house, personal life. There was no place in her world for him.

"How can I ever thank you?" she said, gesturing to her tranquil surroundings, voice husky.

"No need," he replied, chest swelled with satisfaction at having provided not only pleasure but a haven for her during her pregnancy. Margaret would only be a few steps away if help was required. Shoot, for that matter, India would no doubt be a comfort to the older woman, as well. The fit was perfect. Unlike the attraction simmering between the two of them. "Glad I could help."

"There has to be something I can do."

As if thinking, she drew in her lower lip. The sexy-as-hell nibbling frown was almost his undoing.

"I know. How about if tonight I cook you dinner? Somewhere in the back of my SUV is a hibachi. I make a mean steak with mushroom sauce."

He groaned. "Sounds amazing, but I've got reunion stuff tonight." *Which I'd gladly dump in a heartbeat for a few more hours with you.* Trouble was, he'd already proven himself incapable of keeping one woman. India deserved more than the obviously lackluster brand of emotional support he was capable of giving.

"You sure?" she asked. "I don't have all that much to unpack. We could eat early, leaving you plenty of time to meet up with your friends."

Raking his fingers through his hair, Graydon sighed. "I'd love nothing more than to spend the night—well, at least part of it—with you, but I thought we'd agreed to play things cool."

"We have. I merely invited you to dinner—not a makeout session." Her playful elbow to his ribs skewered what little remained of his resolve.

"GRAYDON?" India winced after flipping on the back-porch light. "What are you doing?" Already in her staid white flannel nightgown, she had been hoping for her first bear sighting, when she'd heard a noise outside her door. The last thing she'd expected thirty-five minutes after Graydon had left was to find him lying on the gravel alongside her SUV.

"What's it look like I'm doing?" Following closer inspection, he'd wielded a can of Fix-A-Flat and was holding it up to her left rear tire.

"Okay, maybe the better question is why? That tire was fine when I got back from the grocery store." Barefoot, her long hair neatly pulled into two braids, she gingerly made her way across the deck and down four stairs to where her car was parked.

"That's all well and good," he said, pushing to his feet with a grunt, "but when I left, it was looking a little shady. I ran out to get this—" he wagged the can "—just to get you through the night. In the morning, I'll set you up with the best mechanic in town. He'll then set you up with his tire guy."

"But—"

"A simple thanks will do." He lifted the lid to her bearproof trash container and he tossed the can inside.

"Of course. Thank you, but—"

"If you're going to be a mountain girl, you'll have to learn to be more prepared. There are some mighty desolate places out here where I wouldn't want you or your baby to get caught alone."

"O-kay. I will. Try to be more careful, that is." Unexpected gratitude warmed India to her toes and tightened her throat. Not once in her entire life had anyone remotely cared whether she made it somewhere safely. Oh, sure, maybe Lyndsay. But as evidenced by Lyndsay's casual note, it wasn't as if Lyndsay had been sitting home, fretting over her sister's arrival. "But you don't have to come rushing back in the morning. I can handle getting a tire fixed."

"Did I say you couldn't?" he asked with a throaty chuckle. "After the amazing dinner you fixed, can I not repay you with a little hometown hospitality?"

"Of course. But aren't you supposed to be in that 5-K run in the morning?"

"It'll be over by nine-thirty. I can be out here by ten. Is that too long to wait? Would you rather meet me in town?"

Yes, to both questions.

Trouble was, India's racing pulse told her she should say no. Never had she depended on anyone other than herself. It was safest that way. After all, look where just a few weeks' blind trust in Zack had landed her. She put her hands on her stomach.

"India?"

In the floodlight's harsh glare, she grew inordinately aware of not only Graydon but of her runaway feelings for him. No—not just feelings. Burning attraction. Attraction that was wrong on so many levels, yet felt so right.

"You okay?"

"Yeah," she said with a faint smile and nod. "I'm great."

"Sure? Because just now a sad expression flashed over that pretty mug of yours that looked as if you'd lost your best friend."

"Nah." She grinned and shook her head.

"Hey," he said, voice all soft and tender with concern, "you're seriously worrying me here. What's up?"

In the simple act of taking her hand in his, grazing his thumb across her palm, he crumpled the mental paper on which she'd carefully stated her every objection to why falling for him was a bad idea.

To the accompaniment of chirping crickets and the gurgling stream, and squeezing his hand for all she was worth, India said, "This is going to sound *out* there, but in my whole life, I've never had anyone care whether I had a flat."

"Not even your baby's father?"

She snorted. "Especially not Zack."

"Okay, well, there's a first for everything. So what's the problem?"

"The *problem*," she said on the heels of a strangled laugh, "is that you are far too charming for your own good. I mean, not only did you help set the table, but you cleared it, and even washed dishes while I lounged around eating cookies and reading a movie magazine. Then you skipped out on whatever party you were supposed to go to, to help me out with a tire that *might* go flat."

"And? Say, if I'd invited you to my house and I looked tired from the stress of driving cross-country and lugging a baby around, wouldn't you have done the same?"

His question was so off-the-charts ludicrous, his smile so

dazzlingly big and white, that India couldn't help but smile, too, then crush him in a hug.

The problem?

Oh—it was a biggie. The more time she spent with Graydon Johnson, the more she found herself never wanting to let him go.

Crazy.

And yet…undeniable.

"You're late."

Graydon entered the Silver Cliff Elks Club banquet hall, where his class's cocktail party was to have been held, only to be greeted by his old algebra buddy, Heather Markam. She sat at a vestibule registration table, where his was the only name badge not yet claimed. "Sorry," he said, removing the backing from the *Hello, My Name Is…* sticker and slapping it on his chest. "I didn't realize it was so late."

"That's okay. I would've just abandoned your tag, but it gave me a great excuse not to venture farther." She gestured over her shoulder toward an already rowdy crowd.

"Not a party girl?"

She shrugged. "I like to have a good time, but most folks passed that point about an hour ago. They're now well into the three-sheets-to-the-wind phase, and I'm my crowd's designated driver."

"Ah," he said with a nod. "Know the feeling."

Exhausted from the mere thought of mingling with his tipsy classmates, Graydon briefly shut his eyes.

Big mistake.

What had his mind's eye shown? India. Standing on that back deck. Her old-fashioned nightgown clinging to her long, lean legs. Her barely rounded belly. Her pregnancy-ripe breasts.

About the same time that his mouth went dry, other parts

of him went hard, placing him in the awkward spot of having to manage a face-saving escape.

Snatching one of the yearbook-size pamphlets some industrious classmate had put together, he covered himself, then with a minimum of small talk dived into the party.

He grabbed a Coke and mingled, but as Heather had pointed out, everyone was too far gone to hold a decent conversation that didn't feature overexuberant, manly backslaps or high-pitched feminine squealing.

Wandering out to a concrete patio that had been designated the smoking area, he found Tiffany crushing a butt.

"Thought you'd kicked the habit," he said, moseying her way, enjoying the cooler air and the more muted techno beat.

"I did." She flashed him a grin. "You know what they say about old habits dying hard."

"Sure."

"How've you been?" he asked, surprised to find he genuinely cared.

"Good." Fumbling for another cigarette, she added, "But I miss Jake."

"You know you're welcome to see him anytime."

"I know. But it's tough. I left him. Poor guy's gotta be ticked."

"He was. Is. He loves you, though. He's a great kid. Not one to hold grudges."

Taking a deep drag, then slowly exhaling, she nodded.

"You happy?"

She gazed out at the dark night and shrugged. "Some days I'm not even sure I know the meaning of the word. Others, yeah. I'm on top of the world."

"Do you ever regret…you know…"

"Leaving?"

"Yeah." Because suddenly, he had to find out.

"Truthfully, for a split second yesterday afternoon, I saw you kissing that girl from the Class of 2004 and I was out of my mind with jealousy. But then it occurred to me that I'd had you and thrown you away. Back when I knew you, you were damaged goods. I used to love you more than my own life, but things change. People change. Now…" She turned her attention back to her cigarette.

The old Graydon would have gotten a thrill out of Tiffany's admission that for even an instant, she'd been jealous. But the new man emerging within him was sad. Sad that he'd ever even stooped so low as to pull that kind of juvenile stunt. Saddened further that he'd drawn an innocent like India into his game.

Throat tight, he said, "Sorry."

"For what?"

"Everything. Things going bad. I never set out to hurt you."

"I know. Likewise." She crushed her cigarette, then wrapped him in a hug. He used to find her smoky scent arousing. Now he found it disappointing.

"CONGRATULATIONS!" India called above the cheering crowd as Graydon finished the 5-K charity run.

"Hey, I thought I was meeting you at your place." He jogged toward her. When he reached her, he braced his hands on his knees, catching his breath.

"No sense in you driving all the way out there when I'd have to bring my car in anyway. Besides," she said with a wink she didn't mean to be flirty, "this way, I got to see you all decked out in your running suit."

"My running suit, huh?" He rose to his full height, and the breadth of his shoulders stole her next breath. His gray Silver Cliff Athletic Dept. T-shirt hugged his powerful chest like a second skin, and his red athletic shorts showed plenty of muscle. In a word, the man was *gorgeous*.

And leaving for his East Coast home in the morning. Never to be seen again. What about that fact couldn't she grasp?

"It's a good-looking suit," she said, determined to hold up

her end of the banter. Come Monday morning, she'd have plenty of time for melancholy. Until then, she'd enjoy what little time they had.

"That's because I'm a good-looking guy." He winked.

She actually blushed. To cover, she asked, "How's the rest of your day?"

"You mean schedulewise?"

"Uh-huh."

Side by side they headed for the parking area—no easy feat, considering the size of the jostling crowd. "Brunch, picnic, flag football, prebanquet cocktails, banquet cocktails, actual banquet, dance, postbanquet cocktails, then, if I've managed to live through all that, I might grab an hour's sleep."

"Whoa. Sounds like you'll be a busy beaver."

"Yep, but here's the deal…" Stopping, taking her hands, forming an island in the midst of hundreds of chattering graduates, he said, "What would you say to my skipping all that, and you being my date for tonight's banquet and dance?"

"But…" Standing in brilliant July sun, surrounded by snow-capped mountains and soaring trees and air so clean and crisp it hardly seemed real, India wanted to say yes, yes, yes! with everything in her. So why did the thud in her stomach tell her *no?*

Gee, could it be because she was carrying the baby of a man who'd viewed her only as a temporary diversion, and here she was, already on the brink of another fleeting affair?

"I'm waiting," Graydon said, giving her hands a squeeze. "Please, don't leave me hanging. I feel like some geek who just asked the homecoming queen to prom."

"Hey," she teased, "I *was* a geek, thank you very much."

"Looking back on it, weren't we all. But that doesn't answer my question. Want to be my official date for tonight?"

"Graydon…" She drew her lower lip into her mouth for a nibble. She wanted to agree. She wanted to spend a long, leisurely afternoon soaking in a bubble bath and shaving her legs and doing her nails and hair and immersing herself in the girlie fun she'd missed during her own high school years. But going to this one dance wouldn't erase twelve painfully lonely years of school. Spending more time with Graydon—romantic time circling a dance floor in his arms—wouldn't make it easier to finally let him go. "Thanks so much for the offer, but I've still got unpacking to do, and really, I've already kept you from getting reacquainted with all your friends."

"Gotta say," he mumbled, releasing her hands to shove his fingers through his hair, "out of all the times I've asked women on dates, you're the first to turn me down. It hurts. Really, truly, deep down hurts."

"Graydon, I—" What should she say? Was he going to cry?

"Gotcha!" he teased, flashing her his customary sexy grin. "Seriously, I do wish you'd reconsider, but if you're in a time crunch to get settled before Monday, I understand."

"You do?" Then why didn't *she?*

"Sure. Hopefully, I'll see you around town before I go, but if not, it's been a blast getting to know you."

He pulled her against him for a hug. And she wrapped her arms around his waist, resting her head against his chest. The dry mountain air had evaporated his sweat, and now the only evidence of his recent run was the musky, all-male scent of him. Why was the thought of forever letting him go too painful to comprehend? She hardly knew him, yet—

"Oh. With you snuggled up against me like this, I almost forgot. Didn't we already have a date to get you a new tire?"

"Sure you have time?"

"Absolutely. Do you?"

"Of course. Thanks. Lead the way and I'll tail you." All the while, thanking her lucky stars that this goodbye was only a test run, and that if her luck held out, she'd still have one more hour before his leaving was no longer a drill.

Chapter Five

While standing in warm midmorning sun, waiting for the verdict on India's tire outside Mo's—who was not only the best mechanic in town, but the best chili-dog maker, seeing as how his wife, Monique, ran the chalet-style diner next door—Graydon felt like kicking a tire.

What had he been thinking, asking India to the dance that way? Hadn't he decided cooling things off would be the most appropriate course? She had a baby on the way—had already been badly hurt by her baby's father. What this woman needed was a real man stepping up to the family plate. She needed a guy who'd be there for her and her kid 24/7. And obviously, given that he was headed back to New York Monday morning, that guy wasn't going to be him.

"Now, what we have here," Earl, Mo's tire manager, said in his mountain drawl, "is your classic case of a nail shootin' right through your tread. Pretty big nail, too. This leaves you with two ways to go. Either we can fix your existing tire—a repair that usually lasts fairly well but could open you up for a potential blowout somewhere down the road. Or we could get you a whole new tire. Up to you how you want to go."

"She'll take the new tire," Graydon said. "For safety's sake."

"Do you really think that's necessary?" India asked.

"Hey," he said softly in her ear while Earl got a jumpstart

on the order ticket. "You've got a baby on the way. Can you ever be too careful? This burgh might be all flowers and sunshine this time of year, but once winter rolls around, you'll be grateful to have tackled the issue now."

In the end, she agreed, which left Graydon feeling like a bigger heel. What right had he to interfere in this woman's life—be it in making a decision on tires, or anything else?

"How long will it take?" she asked Earl.

"I'm pretty sure we have this model tire in stock, and the only thing standing between you and your tire's installation is Fred Schmidt's deluxe oil change, so all in all, not more than an hour." Graydon watched while India signed the forms on Earl's busted clipboard. Poor guy, he'd been using the same one for as long as Graydon could remember. Had it duct-taped around the middle. He was the kind of man who could fix damn near anything, be it a car, hot-water heater or his three sons' bikes. Graydon wanted to be like that. A capable, dependable father. Having been married to Brenda for what seemed like forever, Earl was presumably a great husband, too. Everyone always spoke highly of him. As though he was a man you could trust.

And when they speak of me?

Comments from the past came to mind.

"Dude, that guy's insane! Have you seen him throw a reverse half-pipe?"

Or, *"My man Gray here can chug six beers in sixty seconds."*

"I'm sorry," Sheriff Holloway had said to Graydon's folks late one Friday night during his senior year, *"but we had to take in your son for vandalism and underage drinking. You can pick him up at the station."*

Graydon swallowed hard.

"Buck for your thoughts," India said with a playful nudge to his ribs. Earl had gone off in search of her tire.

"A whole buck, huh?"

"Hey, with inflation and all, I figure that's the going rate."

"Probably so."

"Well?" She fished a dollar from her wallet, then offered it to him. "What's up?"

"You got a minute?"

"More like an hour till my car gets done. Why?"

Taking her hand not because he should but purely, selfishly because he wanted to, he led her to his rental SUV. "I want to show you something."

TWENTY MINUTES LATER, India hopped out of Graydon's car only to face yet another breathtaking view. He'd driven to an alpine meadow strewn with tall swaying grasses and wild-flowers in white, yellow and blue. The dirt road had carried them another few thousand feet higher, so that the snowcapped mountains looked close enough to touch and the city of Silver Cliff below resembled a model railroader's make-believe village. Beyond that, the lake she'd last seen sparkle with fire-works now shone mirror perfect in bright sun.

"Wow," India said, her voice nothing in the majesty of their surroundings. "How'd you ever move? I keep pinching myself that I'll actually be living here."

Rounding the SUV's front, he met her, then leaned against the front fender, crossing his arms. His stormy expression didn't reflect the serene view. Jaw hardened, posture stiff, he looked ready to crumble under the weight of his woes.

"I used to think that, too, about living here. How it would literally kill me to move. But life has a way of happening. You know—throws you into a tailspin."

"Why do I get the feeling we're not just here for the view?"

He laughed sharply, grabbed a handful of weeds and stripped their seeds, then scattered them in the wind. "When my dad died—"

"I thought your dad was with your mom. Back in Lake Placid, waiting to pick up Jake from camp."

"He is. But Kent's my stepdad. A great guy and role model. My real dad's here."

It took India but a second to grasp Graydon's meaning.

"He wanted his ashes scattered in this meadow. Said this place was the closest to heaven he'd ever felt on earth."

"It's easy to see why."

"Yeah, well, my dad was kind of the town joke. He was a crap husband and even crappier father. Drank like a fish, smoked like a chimney, cheated on my mom—all-around great guy."

"How old were you when he died?"

"Eight."

"How awful." Truthfully, there'd been times when she'd wondered if she and Lyndsay would have been better off in a foster home than with their father. Which was a huge part of why she was so determined to make a great life for her son or daughter.

Graydon shrugged. "It was one of those mixed-blessings kind of things. Here I was, a kid. Even though, in retrospect, I see what a mess the man was, I still worshiped him. Still wanted him to be like other dads and show up for my school plays or help with homework."

"Sure." How many times had she desperately wished for the same?

"Two years later, Mom married Kent, and we never looked back. It broke Mom's heart to find that the apple of her eye hadn't fallen far from the tree."

"Oh, Graydon, no. What do you mean by that?" Heart aching for this man she hardly knew, yet felt she'd always known, she pressed herself to him. Only the breeze whispering among the wildflowers and firs broke their silence.

"Back there, getting your tire, it hit me. Just what a disappointment I must be."

"Are you nuts?" Backing away, she said, "Look at yourself. You were a professional snowboarder. People around the world must've adored you. Now you teach all that you know. Do you realized how noble that is? You're working hard to provide a home and safety and moral support for your little boy, while his own mom chose the easy way out by taking off for greener pastures. You are the very embodiment of what a man's supposed to be."

She glanced up, to find tears pooling his eyes. In that instant she hated his ex-wife, as well as the father who'd done this to him. Filled him with such doubts and pain. "Seeing that we're practically strangers, this may be inappropriate for me to say, but from what I've gathered, you've made plenty of mistakes, yet you've changed. So when are you going to forgive yourself? Give yourself permission for a fresh start?"

A strangled sound escaped his throat, and then he pulled her to him, crushing her with the force of his pain. But she could handle it. She'd borne her own pain and learned from it. She was strong and willing to share that strength with this fellow needy soul. When his tears finally fell, they were messy and raw, and for the first time since stoically learning of her pregnancy, she cried, too.

And when they'd both quieted, standing there red-eyed and sniffling in an unspoiled alpine meadow, he slid his hands beneath her chin and kissed her. "Thank you."

"For what?"

"Letting me be me. Not laughing at me for not being cool. Not—"

Fingers to his lips, she asked, "How long has it been since you last cried?"

His throaty chuckle spoke volumes. "When my dog, Rudy, got run over by a car. I was seven. When Dad died, at first I didn't believe it. Then I was mad he left. Then I was mad for all the crap he'd done to Mom before he'd left, and then I just shoved it all down deep inside where it couldn't hurt."

"But even that didn't really help?" she probed. "Because it still hurt?"

"Something did," he said with a harsh laugh, tearing up anew. "Guess I just wasn't sure what."

Drawing him into another hug, she said, "Not that I'm a psychiatrist or anything, but did it ever occur to you that all the adrenaline seeking you've been doing, the partying you used to do, was nothing more than that little boy in you trying to escape the kind of pain no child should suffer?"

"My mom's said the same thing."

"And?"

He kissed her nose. "You make a much better case."

"Good."

"I'm sorry though."

"Why?"

"For dumping on you like this. I knew coming out here for the reunion was a mistake. Back home I was finally getting things together. Seeing the old gang, Tiffany..." He shook his head. "It's too much."

"Yet here you are. Not only slaying emotional dragons all over town, but still having time left to save a damsel from housing trauma and a bad tire."

Kissing her forehead, he teased, "I have a feeling you're one damsel quite capable of saving herself."

True. But oh, how India had grown tired of the struggle. Graydon would never understand how much his simple acts of kindness had meant.

"Go with me tonight," he said softly. "I don't want to be alone."

And because she didn't, either, she agreed.

Chapter Six

"India, if you've never ridden before," Graydon's former class-mate, Joanie Euwing, said in between bites of what a silver-edged, ivory menu card described as *filet mignon aux champignons*—apple-wood bacon-wrapped *filet mignon* with a mushroom *bordelaise,* "then you should drop by our stables." She patted her husband, Larry's, shoulder. "My guy here runs the best operation in town."

"I will," India said, still pinching herself not only over the warmth of everyone at her table, but at the splendor of the high-ceilinged ballroom.

"While you're riding," Graydon said with a chuckle, "ask Larry to tell you about the time his horse took off without him."

"Hey," Larry protested, "that wasn't my fault. Smoky Joe was spooked by a chipmunk."

"That may be, but the result was the same. How far did you end up having to walk before Joanie sent out a rescue party?"

While Larry blushed and everyone shared a laugh, it was all India could do to convince herself that she wasn't dreaming. How many nights had she lain awake in bed, dreaming of be-longing? Of having friends and some fairy-tale event to share with them?

"You should smile like that more often," Graydon whis-pered in her ear. "Makes you even more beautiful."

"Thank you," she said, feeling both pretty and complete.

"Having fun?"

"I'm having an amazing time. This is…" Gazing around the room, then back to him, she said, "Thank you for including me in this special night. My father moved us around so much that I never experienced a sense of community like this. One thing I dearly want for my baby is for him or her to have roots. To feel that he or she belongs."

"Silver Cliff's a great place to do just that," he said. "You should be happy here. Both of you."

Was she only imagining the flicker of sadness in his expression? Did he have regrets over leaving his hometown? Or could there be something more? That a part of him wished he were sticking around to watch her happiness unfold?

"Well?" a buxom, chirpy blonde Graydon had earlier introduced as Stephie Dalton inquired. "What does everyone think of my creations?" With a flourish worthy of Vanna White, she gestured to the centerpiece. A three-foot, soaring-eagle-shaped topiary made of mini white and black roses, with a base of trailing English ivy. The bird held a red tulip in his mouth, and the pot containing the arrangement was a silver ice bucket filled with mock-silver nuggets. "It took three days to spray paint all the rocks, and the flowers themselves cost thousands. Can anyone say tax write-off?" She winked.

"It's, um, big," Joanie said.

Larry said, "I'd hate to have that thing fly over me after it'd just had a meal."

Joanie gave him a smack.

"I like it," India said. "Incredibly creative. Do you do lots of work for the hotel? And if so, would you mind giving me your card? It'd be great to hook up with a florist who works well with themed parties."

"I've of course partnered with the hotel in the past, but now that you'll be handling these sorts of affairs, I'd love to start offering more specialty services."

From a red-sequined purse that matched her dress, she withdrew a business card, which India smilingly accepted.

Wow. Here she was making friends and business contacts in one fell swoop. And all, thanks in large part, to the man seated beside her. Sure, she could've eventually found her own way in the town, but just as when he'd introduced her to her landlord and new friend, Margaret, tonight, he'd again in a sense given her his endorsement.

She was ready to burst with gratitude, and tears stung her eyes. Cupping her belly, she acknowledged that from here on, she and her baby would lead a wonderful life. The only bittersweet part was that Graydon would no longer be around to share in it.

"Not to brag," Stephie said, "but I handled the other decorations, as well." Which were equally fun and creative. At each place setting sat a stuffed mountain lion—the new school mascot. Rising from each table in varying heights were at least ten silver helium balloons, lending the room a dreamy, starry-night flair. "I ordered the mountain lions from China."

"Grrr…" Graydon said, picking up his stuffed toy to nuzzle India's neck.

Scrunching, she laughed.

Apparently not to be outdone, Larry's lion also went on a kissing spree—only, straight to Joanie's lips.

A jealous twinge crept through India. Not over wanting to kiss Larry or the lion but Graydon!

"Have I mentioned lately how gorgeous you look in this dress?" Graydon required every ounce of his gentlemanly willpower not to slowly undo the zipper hugging India's painted-on black cocktail dress. Lucky for him they happened to be on the dance floor of his old high-school gym, slow dancing to

The Eagles' "Desperado," surrounded by fellow graduates of all ages.

"I'm lucky it fit," she said, her words warm against his chest. He'd long since ditched his suit coat and tie and now wore his starched cotton shirt open at the throat. "I didn't expect to gain so much weight so fast."

"Are you hungrier than usual?"

She laughed. "When I'm not sicker than usual."

"How're you now?" he asked, loving the feel of her in his arms. Especially loving how he couldn't care less that Tiffany and her Neanderthal danced only a few feet away. Their talk the other night had been freeing. His morning with India at the meadow where his father's ashes were spread had unexpectedly liberated him from a huge part of his past. He hadn't realized how much baggage he'd been carrying around, until he'd left it all on top of that mountain.

"I'm amazed," she said. "Thank you. This has been a wonderful night. Meeting your friends, being such a part of everything—despite having virtually just gotten here…"

She dazzled him with the sheer size and perfection of her toothy grin. A grin that all too quickly faded.

"That said, I do feel guilty."

"About what?" The music changed to a frenetic, hip-hop song. "Hold that thought," he said, hand on the small of her back as he guided her through the crowd.

Outside, beyond a cluster of smokers, beyond a few makeout kings and queens, he found a secluded bench where, save for crickets and the bass beat still pulsing from the gym, it was quiet enough to talk. Nestled at the foot of a grand old Douglas fir he'd carved his initials into, the bench was the same spot where he and Tiff had broken off and made up a dozen times. Tonight, Tiffany was a faded memory, whereas India was a blazing presence.

Her hand in his, he asked, "Okay, now, what has you feeling guilty?"

"The fact that this is your class reunion, yet you've spent most of your time with me, instead of catching up with old friends."

"I'll let you in on a little secret," he said with a sad laugh. "Those friends? Aside from a precious few—like the folks we ate with—I've outgrown."

Wrinkling her cute nose, she asked, "What's that mean?"

"Exactly what I said. The way Jake is too grown-up to still play with Barney? That's how I feel about my old crew. Whereas they're still into hanging out, issuing asinine dares, I'm into raising my kid and earning a living."

"That's all well and good," she said, "but when do you have fun?"

"Gee, thanks. I thought chatting here with you fell squarely under that category."

"You know what I mean."

He played at wincing when her teasing elbow jab landed between his ribs. "At least, we *were* having fun before you attacked me."

She rolled her eyes. "Granted, we're nearly strangers, but you used to be a pro snowboarder, right?"

"Yeah. So?"

"So you were one of the lucky few who figure out how to spend a lifetime doing what they love best. Okay, so Tiffany said you needed to grow up…tend the home fires and all that. But why can't you do both?"

"I don't get the question."

"I'll rephrase. What if it wasn't so much the snowboarding Tiffany hated but the lifestyle accompanying it? Aren't there any straight-arrow-type guys on the circuit?"

"A few. But they're older."

"That's my point," she said, poking him in the chest. "Why'd you have to go cold turkey on a sport you love to prove you've matured? Why couldn't you have taken Jake and

Tiffany along with you? Hired a nanny to homeschool? Granted, it wouldn't have been a traditional lifestyle, but maybe it would've been enough to make your ex happy."

"Why are we talking about my ex?"

She bowed her head. "The way you kissed me the other day—you know, out of the blue—to get back at her. The logical assumption would be that you want her back. If that's the case, I'm trying to help."

And he adored her for that. Funny thing was, a year ago he had wanted to patch things up with his ex, but now, with the benefit of a clear head and hindsight, he saw the cracks in the relationship's foundation that had doomed them from the start. Yes, he'd loved boarding, but he'd also loved his family. He'd wanted Tiff to be home for him, when she'd wanted to be out with her friends. In the beginning, they'd been too much alike. Then, once they'd had Jake, they'd been forced to change. To grow and become responsible parents. She'd resented the changes, while he'd fought to incorporate them into his fast-paced life. Coaching had seemed the safest way to go.

But could he have been wrong? Was there a way for him to have the best of both worlds? To compete *and* have a rich home life by merely taking that life with him on the road, then, during the off-season, making the most of months spent at his Lake Placid home? Spending plenty of time with Jake, his parents and friends?

An image of India flashed before his mind's eye. Her bright eyes and smile. And suddenly, with a painful yearning, he wanted her in the picture, as well. They'd only just now gotten to know each other. It hardly seemed fair that they'd soon be apart.

"What's got you so deep in thought?"

"The usual. Life." He flashed her a faint grin. "Wondering who made that rule about not being able to have your cake and eat it, too."

She laughed. "What kind of cake is it you're craving? I

make a mean red velvet cake with extra-yummy icing. If you'd like, I'll even pack some to go."

"That's just it," he said, sighing. Bracing his hands on her cheeks, he forced her gaze to his. "India Foster, somewhere in the past few days you've become my cake, and I don't want to let you go."

Leaning forward, touching her forehead to his, she said, "I know the feeling. But you have to go."

"And you, having just landed a great new job, have to stay."

Her warm, punch-scented exhalations teased his lips.

He wanted to kiss her.

Bad.

But then what? She had a baby on the way, fathered by some guy who'd loved her and left her. Graydon wasn't willing to be that same love-'em-and-leave-'em type. So what was he supposed to do?

"Ready for me to take you home?"

He released her, to find her eyes big and glistening in the shadows. For as long as he lived, he'd never forget the haunted sight of her, the intoxicating mingling of tangy pine and her light floral perfume.

"I suppose you probably should," she said. "I've got lots to do tomorrow to get ready for my first day at the hotel."

"And I should probably pack and catch up with a few folks I haven't yet seen."

She rose, plastered on what he read as a forced smile.

"Come on, then. With us both so busy, sounds like we should get a good night's rest."

Rest.

Yes, that was all he needed to clear her scent and smile and sweet perfection from his muddied head. But what he really desired was to make love with her till dawn, then wake up only to do it all over again. He then wanted to serve her breakfast in bed. Take her on a long hike into the mountains, and he'd show her his favorite glacial lake, where the water was so glassy and still you could see straight to the bottom; where the trout he'd catch her for lunch would wink straight up at them.

He wanted to do all that. But knew damn well he couldn't. Or would that be *shouldn't?*

Chapter Seven

"You sure know how to make a lady feel special," India teased Graydon while hefting her latest armful of firewood to his pile of smoking kindling.

"Funny," he said with a wink and grin, "but I don't recall seeing any *ladies* on this part of the mountain."

"Beast," she said, dumping her load to pummel his shoulder.

"Beauty."

Snagging her waist, he pulled her in for a breathless kiss, yet again placing her under his spell. For the umpteenth time of the enchanted afternoon, she wondered how could she have met such an amazing guy, only to lose him.

While he caught lunch—a brook trout—from a lake so blue it could've been straight off a postcard, she asked herself what she was doing here relaxing, when she should be finishing her unpacking, and ironing her newly purchased business wardrobe, and studying the packet of hotel stats Emily had given her to check over that weekend. She should be doing all that, but the only thing she seemed capable of was worrying about the ever-growing lump in her throat that worsened every time she thought of Graydon boarding his morning flight.

How had he come to mean so much in so little time? What was it about him that made Zack seem like a boy in comparison?

Gee, could it be that Graydon honored his commitments, whereas Zack had run—literally—an hour after hearing she carried his child?

But playing devil's advocate, Graydon and his wife were divorced. By his own admission, he hadn't been a saint during the course of the relationship. Not that she was even looking for potential husband and father material, but if she were, would Graydon—or even a guy like him—top her list?

She glanced up from the purple wildflower she'd been twirling, to find him messing with their backpacks. "What're you doing?"

"Nothing." Continuing with his task, he flashed her a smile.

When she realized that he was transferring gear from her pack to his, her heart melted a little more. "You don't have to do that," she said as he removed a small camp stove. He'd borrowed it from Larry to bring along for an emergency, as had been the case with most of their gear. That he was so responsible touched her. During the brief downtime she'd had during her stay, she'd read plenty about the mountains' beauty. As well as their hidden dangers. Above the tree line as they were, even in summer, weather quickly changed from sunshine to snow. Hypothermia was a force to contend with. If someone in your hiking party fell, it could take hours—days—for help to reach them. Even knowing all that, though, Mr. Safety, as she'd teasingly called Graydon, had thought of everything to ensure their day's comfort and security. "I'm pregnant, not an invalid."

"I know. But you've got to be tired from the hike up, and after lunch, it's a long way back down."

"Still…"

He dropped the packs, hiking boots crunching the pebbled ground as he strode her way. After kissing the top of her head, he said, "What's the problem with me wanting to pamper you?"

"Maybe the problem is that I can take care of myself."

"Did I say you couldn't?"

"No, but—"

He hushed her latest objection with a lingering kiss. "In case you haven't noticed, I like you. By association, I also like that teeny boy or girl inside you. Altitude's a funny thing. Affects everyone a little different. *Please,*" he said, crouching to cradle her hands in his, "as a favor to me, don't overdo."

"I would've loved to do just that while you had me hauling all that wood."

"Hey, I had to get some work out of you before you conk out on me."

"Who said anything about—" she yawned "—conking?"

Tossing her a thick, red blanket, he said, "I rest my case."

She stuck out her tongue.

On her feet, brushing her backside before spreading the blanket on a grassy patch, she asked, "Care to join me?"

"I would, but someone around here has to cook."

"Glad it's not me," she replied with a happy sigh, lying back to drink in the warm sun. She wouldn't actually sleep, she promised. Just relax a bit before helping Graydon with the rest of the meal prep.

Famous last words…

With the sun casting longer shadows, India awoke to Graydon crooning a nonsensical tune about her waking up. Edging open one eye, she found him, as well as their surroundings, just as dreamy as when she'd drifted off. She'd always been a light sleeper. Never prone to adequately resting in new places. But something about the crisp mountain air overlaid with the delicious scent of sweet wood smoke and their lunch frying in the pan put her at ease. Maybe more to the point, Graydon put her at ease.

How long had it been—if ever—that she'd had the luxury of letting someone else take charge? Her father had been so inept that she'd largely raised Lyndsay. Cooking meals, doing laundry and dusting had all followed homework. Her social life

had been a joke. Which was probably why she'd so readily
fallen for a man like Zack. Out for only one thing—his
pleasure.

How do you know Graydon's not the same?

Truthfully, she didn't. Not factually. Not in the way she
knew the earth rotated around the sun or that water froze at
thirty-two degrees Fahrenheit. But inside…. Deep in her soul
where she held her most closely guarded fears and hopes.
There she knew beyond a shadow of a doubt that, while it
would be impossible for Graydon and her to share anything
beyond this one shining day, he would never hurt her. Not in-
tentionally. No doubt he wasn't even aware of how sharply
saying goodbye to him would cut.

And if he did? Know that despite having been friends only a
short while, she could hardly bear the thought of letting him go.

"You're awfully quiet over there," he said, heaping fish
onto a plate beside a salad and steaming bread. "Still sleepy?"

"I suppose." The statement was a half truth. Since becoming
pregnant, she was always tired, it seemed. But what currently
made her especially weary was yet again having to lose
someone before he'd ever fully been hers. The few times in
school she had made friends, her father had once again moved
the family. By the time she'd reached college, she was pleasant
to her classmates but never went out of her way to engage in
more than surface relationships. What was the point? Especially when, inevitably, it ended in her losing. Losing friends.
Confidence. Hope that her life would ever be filled with more
than deliberately busy days to mask her lonely nights.

"You don't have to eat yet if you don't feel like it. In fact,
if you want, we could just spend the night up here. We've got
enough gear."

Mmm… How tempting the offer was. "What about your
flight?"

"It's not till ten. We'd have to hustle in the morning, but it's doable."

"Uh-huh," she said with a sigh. "What about the fact that my new boss is expecting me to arrive by nine?"

"Emily's a doll. We've been friends forever. One of the benefits of which is that I've got plenty of blackmail material that'll make her gladly ignore you being tardy your first day." He handed India her plate and a fork and napkin.

Laughing, she asked, "Is there any bind you can't work your way out of?"

"WOULDN'T YOU LIKE to know." Though Graydon had kept his reply lightheartedly cryptic, he didn't find it too great a stretch to realize that, sadly, the cold lead in his gut pretty much answered her question. He now was in a hellacious bind he had no idea how to get out of—or even if he wanted out! Considering that he was leaving in the morning, his attraction to India was an ever-growing dilemma.

"Tell me something," he said, dishing out his own meal, then sitting cross-legged on the blanket beside her.

"Shoot."

"That night I discovered your flat tire, you told me no one had ever done something so simple as check out your car for you. How come?"

"Circumstances." Shrugging, she added, "You know how things go." She fisted a pebble from alongside the blanket, then tossed it into the lake.

The glassy surface rippled, forming dozens of rings, reminding him of the inside of a tree. How each ring told a story about the tree's life. Only, in their case, his life was open and India's was locked up tight.

"Actually," he said, taking his first bite of fish, noticing she hadn't touched her plate, "I was pretty lucky to land such a great stepdad. You told me earlier your mom left when you and Lyndsay were little, but what's the story with your father?"

"It's really long and boring. Trust me, you wouldn't be interested."

"Hey—" he set his plate beside him and eased fallen hair behind her ears "—how 'bout letting me be the judge?"

She glanced at her meal, forked a bite of fish, then rested her plate on her lap.

"How many times have you been there for me this weekend?"

"A few."

He laughed. "More like a few dozen. I've been a wreck. And you, a virtual stranger, have been the one helping get my head on straight when here I'm surrounded by supposed friends. Know what that makes me?"

"What?" She finally met his gaze. Her eyes loomed huge, welling with glistening tears.

"That makes me officially indebted. Meaning no matter what ghosts lurk in your closet, I'm obligated to sit here for however long you'd like, hearing each and every boring, horrific, tragic, embarrassing or downright shameful moment."

"There's nothing shameful," she protested. "At least nothing I've done."

Grinning, he said, "I figured as much. Just checking if you were listening."

More than anything, he longed to be there for her the way she'd been for him. More than a few times when he'd been stuck with his old high-school pals, he'd pondered India's mysteries. Such as why a warm, funny, gorgeous, vibrant woman would travel halfway across the country to some town she'd never even been to, determined to set down roots. It was almost as though she was escaping something. But what?

"You really care?" she asked, voice small.

He nodded.

And as she told her story, she broke his heart.

Chapter Eight

"I can't thank you enough for this day," India said well after darkness had cocooned her fairy-tale chalet and the man who was quite possibly the sweetest on earth had walked her to her back door. "The scenery was gorgeous, but…" She glanced down, glad she'd forgotten to leave on the porch light so he wouldn't see her embarrassed expression.

She'd told him *everything.*

About her father's drinking. About their family's constant moves. About her at times desperate loneliness. Most of all, about how she now craved stability and friendship and the peace of mind that came from knowing she belonged, that she'd carved out a special place that was all her own in the world.

Struggling to find adequate words, she said, "What you've done for me in helping me land on my feet after finding Lyndsay was gone. It's…" Her words faded into moonlit shadows. "I can't even explain how fond I've grown of you. Which I suppose is silly, really, but—"

He silenced her with a kiss.

"Graydon, I—"

He did it again. And when he'd thoroughly befuddled her and prevented any cohesive thought from entering her mind, he said softly, "You're an incredible woman. I'm not only honored that you like me, but I feel the same. Trouble is…"

Foreheads touching, they both understood exactly what he referred to and there was no further need to speak. No matter how strongly they might have bonded, he had his son to return to. His job. She had her job. Her pregnancy. They both had hugely full lives that had nothing to do with each other. Yet somehow, in that moment, it felt as if they had everything to do with each other.

"Know what I wish?" she whispered.

"What?"

"That I'd met you before Zack." *That my baby was yours.*

"Me, too. That way, seeing how I want to scoop you into my arms, carry you inside, then make proper love to you, I wouldn't be such a jerk."

"Even if that's what I want, too?"

"Especially because of that." After kissing her forehead, he said, "What kind of man would I be to make love to you when in less than twenty-four hours I might never be with you again?"

Her stomach lurched. "You won't *ever* be back?" She wasn't worth even an occasional visit?

"You know what I mean," he said. "Besides which, in case you haven't noticed, I'm hardly the kind of guy for you. By your own admission, you need—deserve—a traditional, white-picket-fence kind of life. You need a father for your baby. The kind of guy who's home every day by five, helping you change diapers and, later on, work homework math problems. No matter how desperately in the moment I'm wanting to somehow be that guy for you, I can't."

"Why?" Her heart had mistakenly spoken.

"Because, angel, my track record has already proven I'm a mess at these things. Remember that little matter of my already failing at one marriage? How until recently I wasn't even all that great a father?"

"But you've changed. You said so yourself."

"Sure. But I've got a long way to go till I'm worthy of someone like you. You deserve someone who's perfect right out of the gate. In fact, there're a couple of seriously stand-up guys I could introduce you to before I leave town. We could meet for an early breakfast."

"Stop." Fury lined India's heart at his even suggesting such a thing. She was all the more upset with herself for clinging to him when her tight chest told her his every word was true. "You're right. The last thing I need is another man in my life. First Zack, now you…" She bitterly laughed. "Thanks, but I'll fly solo from here."

"No. Really. My friend Jonah runs a ski-rental shop. He's as stable as they come. Goes to church every Sunday. Never touched a drop of booze in his life, but he's not preachy about it. He's a great guy I know you'd—"

"Stop!" Trembling, turning from him to hide her tears, she rammed her key in the lock and hastily opened the door.

"Honey, if you'd just give him a chance. I really believe you and Jonah would hit it off."

"Thanks. But, Graydon…" Flipping on the kitchen, then porch, lights, she said, "The only thing I'd like to *hit* right now is you."

"I'm sorry," he said. "My suggestion must've come out wrong."

"In what sense? That you don't want to see me with another guy or do, or—" Her back to him, India covered her face with her hands. How had this conversation gotten so out of control?

"Hey," he said, cupping her shoulders. "I'm sorry. I'm not sure what I meant. You just can't be hurt. Hell—*I* don't want to be hurt, but…"

Exactly. And in a case like theirs, mutual hurt was inevitable.

"You're right," she said, swallowing the knot in her throat. "I'm sorry, too."

"Do you want me to just go? Would that be best?"

"Do you think it would?"

A sad laugh escaped him. "News flash—I don't have a doctorate in this sort of thing."

"What do you want to do?"

"Stay."

She wanted that, too.

Only, she wanted him to stay in Silver Cliff and never ever think of leaving. Yet he would. He had to get back to his son. She had to launch her new life. Except, she felt her new life had gotten off to a blindingly fun start. When Graydon left, then what? Why did her shiny penny of a future suddenly look dull?

"What do you want?" he asked, easing his hands around her waist.

On her tiptoes, she answered with a kiss.

"YOU CHEATED," Graydon said, re-counting the squares on the Monopoly board India had said Lyndsay had given her for a birthday present over three years earlier. This was the first time it'd ever been used. He'd found the notion crushingly sad. As had been India's all-too-brief call from her sister, who'd been in a rush to try surfing. "Here's where you should be." He landed her top hat squarely in the center of his high-rent district. "That'll be five hundred bucks, please."

"I don't have five hundred bucks."

"Hmm…" he teased. "You realize what that means."

"What?"

"Either I win or, if you want to switch over to strip Monopoly, those earrings will have to go."

"Beast!" she teased right back, pitching a house at him.

"Haven't you already called me that once today?"

"Yes, but in this case it bears repeating."

"Well?" He grinned.

"Well what?"

"What's it going to be? Are we getting naked, or are we starting a new game?"

She hid a yawn. "What time is it?"

"Last batch of popcorn it was a little after three-thirty."

She sighed. "You know what we're doing, don't you?"

"What?"

"Putting off the inevitable."

GRAYDON AWOKE to sunshine warming his bare feet and India's wild hair itching his nose. Her living-room lights were still on, as well as the TV, which currently featured an infomercial on some not-to-be-missed kitchen gizmo. His back throbbed from the slumped position he'd apparently fallen asleep in on the sofa—with the woman he'd realized sometime between beating her at Monopoly and teaching her how to make Rice Krispie treats that he'd fallen in love with—lightly snoring on his chest.

A glance at his watch told him he still had plenty of time to catch his flight, but she had to be at work in barely over an hour.

Having watched as she'd carefully ironed a navy jacket and skirt, then crisp white blouse that was to be her uniform while working at the hotel, he calculated that aside from a shower and breakfast, it wouldn't take her long to get ready. She'd even made a sack lunch, explaining that she was saving her pennies for baby clothes.

She'd told him how excited she was to be part of the renowned hotel's team. She'd told him how she couldn't wait to learn if her baby was a boy or girl. She'd told him that for the first time in her entire life, she didn't wake up each morning with her stomach knotted from dread. She'd shared all that, yet in some sense, nothing at all—at least, none of the important stuff. Such as how she felt about him.

Oh, he got it that she liked him, but he *liked* peanut butter. That didn't mean he'd restrict himself to a steady diet of the gooey treat.

So what did it mean? Was he admitting in the privacy of his own chaotic mind that somehow, over a long weekend, he'd found a woman he could actually envision spending every day of the rest of his life with?

She moaned, rolling slightly in her sleep. Her clean, feminine scent drifted to him and he was lost.

If what he felt for her truly was in the realm of love, then, after having heard her sad life's story, he owed it to her to let her get on with the business of living happily ever after. Silver Cliff was the perfect place to raise a family.

Yeah, but it'll just be her and her baby....

And Margaret, Emily, Joanie and Larry, Stephie, Earl and Mo. Give her a couple weeks, and with her irresistible personality and smile, she'd be friends with everyone in the whole blessed town. Which left him where?

Out of sight, out of mind.

Resigned to the fact that India wasn't some souvenir he could take home to show off to his friends, family and, most important, Jake, Graydon nudged her awake. "Hey, Sleeping Beauty. Time to rise and shine."

"Already?" she asked with another moan, opening only one gorgeous blue eye.

"Sorry, but yep. Party's officially over." For him, the simple statement held a much deeper meaning. He hadn't realized how lonely he'd been until India had reminded him how to laugh—live.

Grinning up at him, she said, "I do feel as if, over the past few days, we've been at a super-fun party."

"Sorry for it to end?"

"Of course," she said, pushing herself upright for a stretch. "But as much as I can't wait to start my new job, I seriously don't want you to go." Head bowed, she sighed. "Why is it that whenever I find one happy thing in my life, I always seem to lose another? How come, just once, I can't have it all?"

His fingers under her chin, he urged her to face him. Silent tears streamed silvery down her cheeks.

"Hey," he said, pulling her close. "None of that. You do have it all. A great house, thanks to me. A great baby—" which a part of him wished were thanks to him. " A great job, thanks to your own brilliant brain. What more could a girl want?"

Though a selfish part of him craved her desiring him, another part was relieved when she didn't. It only would have made letting go that much harder.

"You're right," she said with a messy sniffle, easing away, wiping her cheeks with the backs of her hands. "Pregnancy hormones have me overemotional."

"It's not as if we won't ever meet again. In fact, I've got a couple boarders scheduled to compete here in January."

Ugh. Six months. Might as well be a year. By then, her cute belly would be huge. The town was loaded with bachelors. No doubt one of them would have long since claimed her as his own.

"Sure," she said, standing, then heading for the fridge. "January. That's not long at all. The time will fly by."

"Right." He held back a sarcastic snort. Donkeys were more likely to fly than time spent without her.

Chapter Nine

"Goodbye," India said, giving Graydon a final hug beside her SUV. She wanted so badly to go with him to the airport, but also wanted to make a good impression on her first day of work. *Even more than staying with this man, whom you've quite possibly grown to love, for the final few minutes he's in town?* She swiped her eyes. The baby had turned her into a drama queen. Every emotion was amplified. That was why she'd seemed to have been so wildly happy whenever Graydon was near—not because he was the man she'd secretly hoped to be hers for the rest of her life. The very notion was ridiculous. They were essentially strangers. Plus, she had to get her own head on straight before jumping right into another affair.

"I've always preferred *see you later.* Has a much less final ring."

She clutched him tighter. "Thanks—for everything."

"I just helped you find a place to stay."

"No," she said with a shake of her head. Her tears started again, and no matter how hard she tried being strong, they wouldn't stop. "Th-thanks for sh-showing me there are a few h-heroes left in the world."

"I'm no hero," he said, voice hoarse as if he might be close to tears himself.

"Y-yes," she said. "To me, that's exactly what you've been." On her tiptoes she kissed him once, twice, fiercely on his lips, then cheek. "I've got to go. Don't take this wrong, but I love you."

"How could I take that wrong?" he asked, his eyes also welling. "It's beautiful. I love you, too."

"You do?"

He nodded.

"But you've got Jake," she said.

"You've got your new job."

"We just weren't meant to be." She daubed her eyes and nose with her sleeve.

"I know."

"Me, too." She half laughed. "But that doesn't make it easier."

"Duh."

"I'll always remember you, Graydon."

"Likewise, gorgeous."

"Call me? Just to let me know you got home in one piece?"

"Of course."

Swallowing hard, she nodded, gave him one last kiss and hug, then climbed into her car, fastened her seat belt somehow, hands trembling, and slid her key into the ignition.

At this altitude, the morning was chilly. Light frost dusted the front window. From nowhere—maybe his own car—Graydon produced an ice scraper, and in thirty seconds had her windshield cleared.

She blew him a kiss.

He pressed splayed fingers against the driver's-side window. She touched his hand, imagining his heat.

"Get going," he said, voice muffled, breath fogging outside the car.

She nodded.

"I'll call."

She nodded.

"Go, okay? I don't want you to be late. And truthfully, this hurts too damn bad."

Feeling the same, India blew him one last kiss, then drove away.

CRAMMED IN SEAT 9A of the puddle jumper that would get him across the Rockies to Denver International, Graydon stared out the window. But instead of seeing the majestic snowcapped mountains he'd always loved, he saw India. Laughing and smiling this morning while brushing her hair. For a woman to be so beautiful should be a crime. If it wasn't illegal, how else could he have become addicted so fast?

She'd drawn things out of him no one ever had. For the first time in years, she made him really think about where he was going and where he wanted to be.

Turbulence jolted the plane, and a bit of the ginger ale he'd ordered splashed onto his jeans. He was dabbing it with a napkin, when he glanced at the couple beside him, holding hands, playfully kissing while the guy acted the hero, promising to keep his girl safe.

On the ground, let alone up here, he had no right making her that kind of promise. He couldn't keep her safe any more than Graydon had been able to keep his marriage intact.

It was a good thing he'd left India when he had; otherwise, he might not've been able to leave. Better yet, he might've somehow, someway, poured on every ounce of his once-patented Graydon charm to woo her into heading to Lake Placid with him. No promises, just the hope of maybe a shared bright future. He wanted her to meet Jake and his parents…a few of the kids he coached. He wanted to show her his new world, introduce her to his new friends. Even better, he wanted to show her a few of his old snowboarding moves. A few fresh ones he'd come up with, planning to teach them to his kids.

You're too young to retire.

Phillip's condemnation rang through his head.

Was he? Too young? And if that was true, could he have been as wrong about retirement as he'd been about other things? Like being a bad father—which he now realized he wasn't.

India haunted him, as well. *When are you going to forgive yourself, give yourself permission for a fresh start?*

Ten minutes' brooding later, it occurred to Graydon that his whole life had been about trekking the road less traveled. Snowboarding was hardly the most conventional of sports, and granted, he'd made some rash mistakes in his youth. But now that he was older, and hopefully wiser, why not follow another unexpected path by taking a chance not only on India but on himself?

Wondering if India would be on board with his plan, Graydon waved over the leggy, redheaded flight attendant, his heart racing.

"Yes, sir?"

"When's the next return flight to Silver Cliff?"

"We'll be in Denver an hour before turning around. Forget something?" She smiled.

He smiled back.

If she'll have me, yeah. I forgot to grab hold of my future wife.

"LONG TIME NO SEE," the Silver Cliff car-rental agent called out as Graydon approached her desk. He'd known Dawn since she'd been a kid. His first girlfriend, Heidi, had babysat for her. "Thought you just flew out."

"I did, but now I'm back—" Ready to toss his cookies from nerves. He and India had just been up all night, deciding that the two of them as a couple would never work. She carried another man's baby. He still carried demons from his first marriage. Then there was Jake. What if he didn't like India?

Graydon shook his head and grinned. What wasn't there to like about India?

"You okay?" the recent Silver Cliff High graduate asked. "You don't look so hot."

"I'm good," he said. "At least, I will be if you still have my car."

Frowning, checking a computer screen, she said, "Sorry. The model you had is already checked out. I do have one compact left. Yellow, okay?"

As long as India didn't laugh him out of her office for being crazy, moonbeam purple would be okay. She had to say yes. Had to. Otherwise…

Well, he wasn't sure what he'd do, seeing as how there was no plan B.

Which was why, being the dork-in-love that he was, he planned on making the entire trip to the hotel with his fingers crossed.

On the way out to his car, he eyed a girlie-pink display window in the airport's only gift shop. In it, along with fluffy pink feather boas and glittering tiaras, was an array of jewels. Necklaces, earrings, bracelets, but, most important—rings. Lots of them with huge, gaudy stones. After debating between the at least twenty-carat emerald or diamond, he instead went with the sapphire toy ring, figuring it matched India's eyes.

"Who's the lucky lady?" elderly Maxine Paulson, a notorious snoop, asked while ringing up his purchase.

"Nice try," he said, "but I never kiss and tell." He winked, then snatched his bag.

"THESE ARE PAST-CLIENT files," Emily patiently explained. "We get a lot of repeat business, so it's always a good idea to keep every scrap of info you compile on any given job. Say, for example— You okay?"

"Huh?" India glanced up from wringing her hands. "Oh—

I'm good—great. Where were you? Files? Repeat customers, right?"

"Right, but why do I get the feeling you'd rather be somewhere else?"

Because I would? Why, India lamented, when she'd waited her entire life for this day, a day when she'd been gifted with a fresh start, couldn't she focus on anything but the pain of that lonely *see you later* remark from a man she hardly knew?

"India?" Emily nudged her shoulder. "This wouldn't have something to do with a certain hunky graduate you were reported dancing with, would it?"

"I don't know," India said with a shrug. Outside, there was another flawless mountain day. Bright blue sky. Cotton-ball clouds. Storybook perfection, and yet here she stood with a lump in her throat the size of Montana. "I guess. Maybe."

"Maybe?" The boss raised her eyebrows. "Either you like the guy or you don't. What's it going to be?"

"Of course I like him. I mean, who wouldn't? He's gorgeous, funny, warm, caring, compassionate…"

Rolling her eyes, Emily teased, "Where do I get one of those all for myself?"

"That's the problem. This particular model happens to reside in Lake Placid."

"As in New York?"

"Yep."

"Oh." Landing in her desk chair with a thud, Emily said, "I didn't realize he'd moved that far. I see where that could be troublesome if you invited him to stop by for video night and pizza. Sorry." She gave India's arm a sympathetic rub. "On the bright side, Silver Cliff's loaded with hot guys."

"That's what he said."

"He thinks it best you date other guys?"

"Well…" Dropping into her own cream leather desk chair,

India scratched her head. "He said he did, but I didn't for a second believe him."

"Yeah. Guys are funny that way. Mark asked me to marry him three times."

"Because you turned him down?"

"Heck no. He kept assuming I'd change my mind. Considering his habits of leaving his dirty clothes and dishes all over the house, maybe I should've taken him up on his offer, huh?"

After sharing a laugh, India sighed. "How long have you been married?"

"It'll be eighteen years in May. Hard to believe," she added with a wistful smile.

"So would you?"

"What?"

"Go back if you had the chance?" Because suddenly India was consumed with the notion that maybe if she hadn't been so determined to set down roots in Silver Cliff, there might've been a chance for her and Graydon. Or was the thought as much a fantasy as the entire weekend had been? Just a lovely dream that—

"Knock, knock."

India glanced up, only to have her heart skip a beat. Standing at the office door was Graydon in all his rugged glory. "Did you miss your flight?"

"Nope," he said, handing her a bouquet of red and black roses. A trio of silver eagles had been affixed with silver picks. "I caught my first flight, then had time to take another. Sorry about those," he said, gesturing to the black roses. "On my cell, I asked Stephie to make them school colors—you know, an inside joke about how you and I met. But these didn't turn out quite the way I'd expected."

Emily coughed. "Would you two like a moment alone?"

"Oh, hey," Graydon said, extending his hand to hers. "Nice

to meet up with you again. And if you wouldn't mind, some one-on-one time would be great."

Alone, India had to remind herself to breathe.

What did this mean? Graydon showing up like this, when by now he could've been most of the way home.

"Wow," Graydon said, wiping his palms on his jeans. "This seemed a lot easier in the planning stages."

"It might help if you let me in on what you were planning," she said, thankful her voice had worked past the knot of hope in her throat. He loved this town. Had he decided to move back? Raise his son where he'd grown up?

"Right. Good tip." Parking on the edge of Emily's desk, he cleared his throat. "On the first leg of my flight, I did some thinking."

"About us?"

He nodded. "But plenty of soul-searching about me, as well."

"And?" She was almost afraid to ask.

His faint smile didn't indicate much. But then he reached for her hands and gave her a reassuring squeeze. His stare met hers, quickening her pulse all the more. "I found that for the past few years I've done a lot of acting."

"Oh?"

"Dropping out of everything I love, in what I now recognize as a futile attempt to be some kind of superdad. Perfect stable job and home and—" he shrugged "—I don't know what I'm saying. I guess maybe that this crazy hurricane of a relationship of ours has shown me there's no such thing as predictability when it comes to love. Be it my love for Jake, or my love for you."

India's pulse raged. Where, where was this going? Where did she want it to go?

"Anyway, I guess what I'm trying to get at in a not-so-understandable way is that my whole life, I've followed the path less chosen and made out like a bandit. For a while, before Tiffany told me otherwise, I was happy. Looking back on it, I realize I've always been a damn good father to Jake—best I could be. Love isn't contingent upon a place but upon the people you're with. And… This might be presumptuous, but it occurred to me that in your own quest for love, you kind of got the same screwed-up message I did. You know, that kids have to grow up in some picket-fence-enclosed house in the same town going to the same school, with the same friends forever. And while I'm not knocking that, I'm just saying there are alternative ways to live. That as long as we have each other—"

"Graydon?" She nudged him. "Out with it. What are you really trying to say?"

"God's honest truth?" he asked, ducking his head, bringing the tips of her fingers to his mouth for a tender kiss. "That I want to return to competitive snowboarding. I want to feel alive again, instead of just going through the motions of life. I want to laugh and have fun and ditch this horrible feeling that if I'm not always uptight and focused on responsibility, I'm somehow doing things wrong. Most of all, I want to be with you. And Jake and the little boy or girl inside you. I want to have my cake and eat it and lounge in it, too—or however the hell that expression goes. I don't know how I fell for you so fast, but I did. And if you feel even a fraction of what I'm feeling, then I say let's go for it. Let's throw caution to the wind and—"

"What are you saying? That you want me to come live with you? Or are you and Jake moving in with me?"

He released her hands to place an adorably gaudy little girl's sapphire ring on her ring finger. "I'm saying that I want you with me. *Forever.* I love you. Yes, we'll no doubt have some growing pains, but what couple doesn't? Marry me."

"But my job?" India said, mouth dry. "The lease on my new house. There's so much I still have to do. I refuse to let this child grow up the way I did, without a sense of family or purpose or—"

"Stop," Graydon said with a quick yet fervent kiss. "Listen to yourself. You're sounding as uptight as me about the whole parenting gig. First off, yes, I want you to quit your job. Come with me to Lake Placid, where, if you like, I'll help find you a new job at another great hotel. Or you can tour with me. Jake, too. If you want, there are probably some great jobs within the U. S. Snowboarding Association. As for your lease, Margaret will understand."

Sighing, hands to her temples, India felt her mind racing as fast as her heart. "I love you, but I had everything planned. The baby and I were going to live here in Silver Cliff. I have this great job, but somehow, even a position as fulfilling as this feels dull compared with the thrill of being with you. And now you throw this great offer on the table. Zack—he…" Her eyes pooled. "He wanted nothing to do with me. How come you're just the opposite? How do I know that when the going gets rough, you won't leave me, too?"

"How do you *know?*" he asked, snagging her waist. "Because I promise to always be a great husband to you, and father to your son or daughter."

"But you once made that same promise to Tiffany."

"Get this straight," Graydon said. "She left me. And Jake. I was willing to make things work. She wasn't."

"Then you still love her?"

He sighed. "What do I have to say to convince you this is right?"

"I don't know," she said, fingers at her suddenly throbbing temples. Everything in her heart screamed to take Graydon up on his offer. Together, they'd lead an amazing life. "I just don't know. How will I fit in with your friends? I've never fit in anywhere. I've always been the outsider."

"Did you feel part of things Saturday night?"

"Yes, but only because you made people be nice to me."

"Are you nuts? Look how quickly everyone here at the hotel has fallen for you. Margaret and Stephie and Joanie. That has nothing to do with me and everything to do with you. You're a sweet, smart, beautiful, amazing woman. Or, in classic boarding terminology, your worries are bogus. The fact that up until now you've led an unconventional existence is part of what makes us a perfect match. Admittedly you've had a rocky life. Please now allow me the privilege of being you and your baby's soft place to fall."

Laughing, crying, India wholeheartedly agreed.

A REUNION ROMANCE
Ann Roth

Dear Reader,

In a short story there's not much time to start a romance! In telling Holly and Brady's story I had to cut straight to the chase. What better way than to reunite them at a high school reunion? And what better place and time than Silver Cliff, Colorado, on the Fourth of July?

But that's not all. You'll meet Holly's cute daughter, her mother and a host of other characters who keep this novella hopping.

I hope you enjoy reading about Holly and Brady, and the other two stories in this anthology, too.

Happy summer and happy reading!

Ann Roth

To Rachael, Stephanie and Katie—
the most wonderful daughters a mother could want.
I am so proud of each of you.

Chapter One

"What a perfect day for a birthday!" As Holly Stevens spread a paper tablecloth over her end of the concrete picnic table at Silver Cliff Park, she smiled at her beaming daughter. "Happy birthday, Alix."

"Happy birthday," echoed Holly's mom while she covered the other end of the table.

Holly's best friend, Aileen, Aileen's husband, Bill, and their son and daughter added their best wishes.

"Thanks, everybody!" Unable to sit still, Alix flashed her dimples and twirled around, the skirt of her pink cotton dress billowing around her.

Holly had wanted her to wear pants, but Alix had insisted on the dress. True, it was summer and, with the bright sun and deep blue sky, already hot. But living in the mountains of Colorado, you never knew what might happen weatherwise. The temperature could drop precipitously within minutes.

"And happy birthday, 'merica," Alix added, twirling again.

"That's right," Holly said. "Today is the Fourth of July. Aren't you lucky to be born on such a special day?"

Alix nodded, then stopped spinning and sobered. "Am I bigger now, Mommy?"

Holly stroked her chin and pretended to study her daughter.

"You certainly are. The girl who was three yesterday is long gone. You definitely look four. Everyone thinks so, right?"

Vigorous nods and smiles around the table pleased Alix. Proud, head high, she took her place at the table.

The park was packed for this year's barbecue, the first event of a four-day weekend that started with the picnic and continued with fireworks. After that there were other events, including an all-years high-school reunion. Eighty-year-old Silver Cliff High School, Holly's alma mater, soon would be converted into condos, with Bill's company the architects. Some seventy years' worth of graduates, scattered over the country and the world, had returned to Sliver Cliff and booked rooms for the last-ever reunion held in the building.

Silver Cliff was packed with visitors—a boon for the tour business—but even with avid hikers and summer vacationers, summers generally were slower than the winter ski season. Not this weekend. For once even the Silver Cliff Lodge, where Holly's gift shop was located, was full. The shop was sure to do a booming business. Which meant extra money. Life was good. For the moment.

If only Mr. Webb wasn't about to sell the lodge to the Treat Yourself Resort chain, also known as TYR. But he wanted to sell, and sometime in the next ten weeks he'd finalize the deal and sign the papers, a move that would put Holly and a good number of employees on the street.

Holly knew her shop could survive if she moved it, but with the tourism businesses booming, there weren't any retail vacancies in town. For anyone lucky enough to find space, the rent was sky-high. Holly had no idea how she'd find a new home for the shop, let alone afford the move or the rent.

For a moment worry darkened her mood, but this was Alix's birthday and the Fourth of July, and no time for low spirits. She forced a smile. "Before we open presents, I'd like to visit the ladies' room. Anyone want to come along—Alix, Kirby, Kelly?"

All three children shook their heads. Holly's mom moved beside her. "I'll go with you."

"Hurry back!" Alix said.

"We will."

As they made their way past friends and families and called out greetings, Holly's mother glanced at her. "In all the excitement I haven't mentioned that you look very nice today. I love that new slacks outfit, and your haircut is wonderful."

"Thanks." Holly touched her hair, highlighted and styled yesterday. "I'm glad you like it."

Given the fact that soon she'd be without a space for the gift shop, spending money at the hair salon and on the new outfit had strained her budget. But after finally shedding the last of the twenty pounds gained during her pregnancy, she'd deserved a reward.

"I hope we'll run into Brady Cornell," Holly's mother said with a canny expression. "How about you?"

Holly rolled her eyes. "Puh-leese, Mother. Brady and I were over a long time ago."

She hadn't even seen Brady, who lived in Denver, nearly two hundred miles away, since the ten-year reunion four years ago. At the time she'd been nearly nine months pregnant and feeling like a lopsided beach ball. Brady, buff and as handsome as ever, had arrived with a glamorous blonde who couldn't seem to take her claws off him. As if Holly were a threat. Which, since their relationship had ended the week before senior prom and they'd barely spoken since, was ridiculous.

"Besides, he's the one putting together the sale of the lodge to TYR." Everyone in town knew that. "Thanks to him, I'll soon be out on the street."

"That's not his fault, honey. The lodge has been for sale a long time. If TYR hadn't made an offer, the place would've shut down. Either way, you'd have to move the shop."

"Maybe so, but I'm still upset." And scared. What if she couldn't find another space?

She needed to keep the shop running to support Alix and help her mom. They shared a sunny, château-style duplex that had once housed vacationing skiers, Holly and Alix in one two-bedroom unit, her mother in its mirror image next door. It was a symbiotic relationship—her mom babysat Alix while Holly worked, making child care worry free, and Holly paid her enough to help make ends meet.

She intended to tell Brady this, and ask him to do something, anything, to help her and the other people working at the lodge. That was why she wanted to see him. And also to show him how good she looked. She wasn't sure why that mattered, but it did.

Would he be here today, or show up tomorrow? Though his family no longer lived in town—his parents had moved to Phoenix and his sister lived with her husband and kids in Alaska—he had plenty of friends here to visit. Holly wanted to search for him, but not with her mother scrutinizing her every move.

She nodded at the sparsely crowded food tent, where local restaurants sold fried chicken, barbecue pork, coleslaw, potato salad and soft drinks every Fourth of July. "We should think about lunch soon, before the line starts."

"It's way too early," her mom said. "Let's wait till after Alix opens her presents. You used to love celebrating your birthday with your dad and me, remember?"

Holly's father, a newspaper reporter, had died of a heart attack when she was fifteen, and she and her mother still missed him. She nodded. "He made my birthday and the holidays such fun."

"Didn't he?" Her mother sighed. "Poor Alix is missing out. She needs a father. Wouldn't it be nice if you and Brady—"

"No, it would not." Holly strode into the park restroom, wrinkling her nose at the disinfectant smell.

While she agreed with her mother, Brady Cornell was not the male she envisioned in the daddy role. She wanted someone ready for a lifetime commitment to her and Alix, not a man others referred to as a babe magnet. A man whose hotel chain gobbled up other hotels, then laid off employees and refused to renew the leases of shop owners who rented space. Those kept on the payroll earned among the lowest pay and benefits in the industry.

No, Brady wasn't for her. Yet she couldn't help wondering what striking woman he'd bring to this year's reunion.

"Well, I always liked Brady," her mother continued as they washed their hands. "He was such a nice boy, and you two were so perfect together. Do you think he's gotten fat now that he's out of pro football?" she asked over the hiss of the water.

"He only played the one year, remember?" Straight out of college, with his attractive then wife to keep him company. "He wasn't heavy four years ago," Holly added. Not at all. He'd been as fit and handsome as ever. "So I doubt—".

"Holly, hello!" said a women she didn't recognize. "Regina Forbes Chase, Class of '90."

Happy for the interruption, Holly exchanged greetings with the woman. Then she and her mother left, the subject of Brady Cornell forgotten.

As HOLLY AND her mother headed for the picnic table she caught sight of Brady. At six foot five, he was easy to spot. He was with Mickey Rennant and Mickey's wife and kids, who lived in town, and they were headed for a table on the other side of the park. Dressed in snug jeans, a chambray shirt stretched across his broad shoulders, the sun on his face and a breeze ruffling his dark, longish hair, he was as hunky and sexy as… Sin.

"There's Brady," her mother said, nodding at him.

"Oh?" Heart thudding, Holly feigned nonchalance.

Suddenly, as if he felt their stares, he glanced over his shoulder. Elbowed Mickey, stopped and pivoted. His gaze hooked Holly's, penetrating enough to still a woman's thoughts. She forgot that she should look away. Her body began to hum.

"He's as attractive as ever, isn't he? And he appears to be alone. He's staring at you!"

"Yes," she replied dreamily. Then caught herself. "But I'm not interested. At all. So don't go getting ideas."

"Of course not."

Her mom gave a knowing smile, which Holly ignored. She nodded at Brady, who nodded back. She would talk to him about the lodge. But not today.

They were about fifty feet from their table when Alix raced toward them, pigtails flying.

"Hurry up, Mommy and Nana," she called, nimbly weaving around adults and children. "It's time to open my presents!"

"All right!" Laughing, Holly pushed Brady from her thoughts.

"HOLLY LOOKS GOOD," Mickey said.

"She sure does." *Hot,* Brady thought as he watched her hurry toward her picnic table. But then, she always had, even nine months pregnant. He glanced at her mom, who wasn't bad, either—Holly was going to age well—and then at her daughter, a cute little imp who couldn't take a step without dancing. The girl's father, who sounded like a real jerk, wanted nothing to do with her.

Through the grapevine Brady knew Holly was looking to get married. He'd tried that once, right after graduating from college and signing a pro-football contract. The marriage had lasted as long as his career, about a year.

Holly hadn't smiled, only nodded, but with TYR about to buy the lodge, she probably didn't want much to do with him.

Brady wasn't thrilled about the lodge situation, either, but his company had decided on the property, and since he was the acquisitions guy…. Once he completed this sale his boss had promised him a big promotion, which would put him in line as the next CEO. Sometime in the next five to seven years, the job was his.

Brady wanted that. He wanted his own chain of hotels, and as CEO he'd have it. For now, like it or not, his job was to close the deal on the lodge. He would explain everything to Holly and make her understand. But not today and not this weekend. After the reunion.

"You gonna talk to her?" Mickey asked.

He ought to say hello. "Yeah. You go on. I'll find you."

As he headed toward Holly, a female hand grasped his biceps, stopping him.

"There you are," purred a voice near his ear. "I've been looking all over for you."

Brady turned to see Monica Combs. They'd been in the same homeroom all through school. He hadn't liked her then and wasn't interested now. Big breasts aside, she was needy and clingy, and wore too much perfume. Stifling a grimace, he peeled her fingers off his arm. "Hey, Monica. What have you been up to?"

"I'm a Realtor now," she said. "Business is booming, but you already know that. If you ever decide to move back to town, I'm your girl." She winked. "I can even presell you a condo in our old school. They're gonna be beautiful. Here, I'll give you my card." She fished into her purse and pulled one out. "I'll jot down my private number on the back," she murmured, fluttering her lashes. "In case you need to reach me."

Brady knew exactly what she wanted, and it was more than a real-estate sale. No, thanks. A dozen yards away Mickey and his family had found a table. Brady gestured at them. "Mickey's waiting for me. Catch you later, huh?"

Monica pulled her lips into a pout. "I hope so."

When Brady glanced at where Holly and her mom had been, they were gone.

Chapter Two

Two hours later, after Alix had opened her presents and the kids had raced around the playground at the edge of the park, Holly, her family and friends were ready to eat.

Aileen squinted toward the lines snaking from the crowded food tent. "We shouldn't have waited so long."

Holly shot her mother an I-told-you-so look. She shrugged. "Maybe we should hold off on food till the entertainment starts."

Every Fourth of July, local theater groups and schoolkids entertained townspeople with songs and theatrical skits. Holly had done that herself, and someday Alix would, too.

"But I'm hungry now, Mommy," Alix said.

"Me, too—" "Uh-huh—" Bill and Aileen's kids chimed in.

"I don't mind the crowds," Bill said. "I was a waiter in college. I can handle a few plates. I'll get the food."

Aileen smiled at her man. "Isn't he a gem?"

As much as Holly loved Aileen and liked Bill, she couldn't stifle a pang of envy. Oh, to have a man in her life who loved her and Alix as much as Bill loved Aileen and their kids. He must be out there someplace, but so far, she hadn't found him.

"Former waiter or not, Bill can't juggle seven plates." She arched her brows at her mother. "If you watch Alix, I'll help."

"I'll watch all three children," her mother offered. "You big kids go on."

Holly, Aileen and Bill headed off, passing families sprawled on blankets or seated at picnic tables. They waved at some, and Bill and Aileen stopped to chat with others. Intent on feeding her hungry daughter, Holly continued alone, all the while studiously avoiding a glance across the park to where Brady was. By the time she took her place in the food line she'd lost sight of Bill and Aileen. She'd have to juggle the plates for her mother, Alix and herself without help.

As the line inched forward, she couldn't help thinking about Brady. She really ought to say hello and get it over with. Just a casual "It's been a long time, and we need to talk later about the pending sale between TYR and the lodge." Then they'd go their separate ways and—

"Holly?" said a male voice behind her.

A voice she knew as well as Alix's. Brady Cornell. Speak of the devil. Her heart fluttered and her stomach tensed. Pasting a casual expression on her face, she turned toward him. "Hello, Brady," she said, sounding breathless to her own ears.

"I tried to catch up with you earlier, but you disappeared."

His deep baritone voice thrummed through her, and his espresso-brown eyes, which always affected her so, emptied her brain of thought. She forgot all about Alix wanting lunch and that soon she would lose her lease. She forgot everything. "Oh," she said, wishing she could come up with a clever remark.

"You look good." His eyes glinted as he looked her over appreciatively. "Really good."

That he liked what he saw pleased her greatly and made the past few months' diet and stationary-bike regimen worth the trouble. Inside, she glowed. Outside, she managed a cool smile. "I would hope so, since the last time we saw each other I was huge. Tell me, Brady, what's the official date TYR takes over the lodge?"

The warmth faded from his eyes. "We're still working out the details, but if things go as planned, sometime late this summer."

"You do know that when that happens, I'm out on the street. So are some of my friends."

He shifted his weight, shoved his hands into the pockets of his jeans. "I'm sorry."

The apologetic expression on his face matched the words and bolstered Holly's hopes. "Then surely there's something you can do."

"TYR wants the lodge," he said. "Without our offer it'll close its doors. Wouldn't you rather it stay open?"

Her mother had asked the same question earlier. "Of course I would. Call me a silly optimist, but I know there's some other way to save the lodge and all the jobs that are going away."

"If there is, I don't see it."

With a sinking feeling, Holly glanced at her family. To her dismay, her mother was watching her and Brady with interest. She groaned.

"What?" Brady followed her gaze. Her mother waved at him and he raised a hand to wave back.

"Don't do that." Holly grabbed his arm. His very muscular arm. Unwanted warmth flooded her. She dropped her hand.

"What's the deal?" he asked, confused.

"Just don't."

"Okay." He shrugged and smiled, instead. Then nodded at Alix, Kirby and Kelly. "Don't tell me you have three kids now."

Holly shook her head. "Two of them belong to Aileen and Bill. The girl in the pink dress is mine."

"She's cute."

"Thanks. She turned four today."

"An Independence Day baby, huh? I'll bet she likes that."

"She does. Nobody else gets fireworks on her birthday." She bit her lip. "I'm trying to give her a good life, Brady."

He scrubbed a hand over his face. "With tourism growing, your gift shop will thrive no matter where you move it."

"Have you checked out the vacant retail spaces lately?

There aren't any." The people in front of Holly and Brady inched forward, and so did they. "Even if I do find a place, the rents are unbelievably high."

"Are they?" With a regretful expression he shifted his weight. "You're a smart, resourceful woman, Holly. You'll figure out something. Maybe a different line of work."

"I majored in English," she said, wishing she'd chosen a different field. "I suppose I could flip burgers or find a receptionist job. But I love running my own shop."

They were almost at the tent. She glanced around for Aileen and Bill, and waved them over.

"There you are." Aileen looked curiously from Holly to Brady, no doubt noting their somber faces. Loyal friend that she was, she frowned. "Well, well, if it isn't the man in charge of the TYR-lodge deal. Hello, Brady."

Bill, himself a businessman, gave his wife a be-nice look, then held out his hand. "It's been a while."

Suddenly the wind whipped up, as if Mother Nature, too, disapproved of the sale.

Holly at last reached the tent. She piled food onto three plates. "Well, I should take this to my family before it gets cold. Can you carry one of the plates, Bill?"

"No problem." He nodded at Brady. "Glad I ran into you, bud. How long are you in town?"

"I leave Sunday afternoon, but I'll be back and forth over the rest of the summer."

"You staying at the lodge?"

"Yeah." Brady rubbed the back of his neck and winced. "See you later."

"Between the fireworks and reunion activities, no doubt," Bill said.

Juggling two plates, Bill and Aileen beside her with five more, Holly started for the table.

Now that she'd talked to Brady, she wasn't sure she wanted

to see him again. He couldn't help her, but her body didn't seem to care.

Darned if she wasn't as attracted to him as always.

LATER THAT NIGHT, while Alix, who had napped during the lull between the afternoon's festivities and now, waved a sparkler in the twilight and squealed with delight, Holly and her mother sat nearby on a plaid wool blanket.

Dozens of children throughout the huge meadow surrounding Canyon Lake repeated the activity, and a haze of smoke floated through the air. In the distance, at the edge of the lake, a group of men worked to make sure the fireworks were ready. The mountain lake, which was a good twenty miles from town, drew families from Silver Cliff and several neighboring areas for an evening of spectacular fireworks.

Yet Holly had never seen such a crowd. Alumni and their families, in town for the reunion, she guessed. There were so many that the reunion committee had hired school buses to transport them.

Alix's sparkler fizzled out. She tossed it onto a pile of used sparklers, then hugged herself. "Brrr, it's cold."

"Canyon Lake is always chilly at night," Holly said, glad she'd convinced her daughter to trade her dress for a warm shirt and pants. "You need your jacket." She rummaged through a bag and pulled out Alix's quilted blue parka. "Put that on and zip up." Alix did, and Holly added, "The fireworks won't start for a while, so how about another sparkler?"

As she reached for the box, she glanced around. So many people. Who would Brady sit with tonight?

"He'll be here," her mother said.

"Who?"

"You know who—Brady Cornell."

Her mother had mentioned his name several times since the picnic. Holly had shared their conversation about the lodge and had done a good job pretending she wasn't attracted to him. She had no interest in repeating herself tonight. She had no interest in Brady, period. "Shall I light your sparkler?" she asked Alix.

Alix turned her attention to the clearing nearby, where dozens of kids twirled sparklers. "There's Jason and Felicia and Kenisha. Can I do it with them?"

"Sure," Holly said. "That'll be fun."

As she stood, her mother pointed straight ahead. "Oh, there he is. Yoo-hoo, Brady!"

Holly cringed. He was with two of the guys he'd played football with, Todd Roberts and Jeff Langston, both divorced. He said something to his friends, then left them and strode forward. For a large, solid man he moved with a fluid grace that made watching him a pleasure. Holly caught her breath. No man should look that good in jeans and a fleece vest.

"Come on, Mommy, let's do the sparklers with Felicia and Jason and Kenisha," Alix said, tugging her hand.

"In a minute." She wasn't about to leave her mother alone with Brady.

Looking a tad wary, he nodded at Holly, then at her mother. "Hello, Mrs. Stevens. It's been a while. You haven't changed a bit."

"Thank you, Brady." Though it was growing dark, Holly thought her mother flushed. "You have. You're grown from a boy into a handsome man. Holly was just saying that she'd love it if you joined us for the fireworks."

"I did not!" Holly said, sounding to her own ears like a petulant teen.

"Who are you?" Alix craned her head upward and stared.

"An old friend of your mom's. Brady Cornell." Brady hunkered down and held out his hand.

"Mommy?"

"You can shake his hand. It's okay."

With big eyes and a sober face, Alix shook. "Hello, Mr. Cornell."

"Happy birthday. Is all this fun for you?"

At the mention of her big day, she brightened. "My cake and presents were. Mommy and Nana gave me an American Girl doll. I left her at home 'cause I don't want her to get dirty. We're also celebrating 'merica's birthday."

"Ah."

"Why don't I take Alix to do her sparklers," Holly's mother said.

Leaving Holly alone with Brady? She shook her head. "You don't—"

"I want Nana to take me," Alix said in a firm voice.

Holly's mother looked pleased. "There isn't much time before the fireworks start, so let's hurry." She flicked on a penlight, then aimed it at Brady. "We really would love for you to enjoy the fireworks with us. Say goodbye to Mr. Cornell, Alix."

"Bye, Mr. Cornell."

Holly's mother and daughter hurried off, leaving her alone with Brady.

ALONE WITH HOLLY, Brady shifted his weight. In the growing darkness around them, families laughed and talked, but she didn't say a word. She radiated tension, all of it directed at him.

Well, hell. He scratched his jaw and searched for something to say. "Your mother's pretty obvious," was all he could think of.

She responded with a tight smile. "It's embarrassing."

Then she glanced at the plaid blanket spread over the ground beside her. After several seconds Brady realized she wasn't going to speak again. He hated that she was angry with him.

Normally he was a private man, but there was no place else to talk, and things needed to be said. "You're gonna stay mad at me about the sale, aren't you?"

Her eyes glittered. "I can't help it, Brady. If things were reversed and you were in my shoes, wouldn't you be upset?"

As he thought about that, he stared at his sneakers. "Yeah, I guess I would. But we're going to see a lot of each other this weekend, and this is our last reunion at Silver Cliff High. For old times' sake, we ought to agree to get along through Sunday." For some reason that was important, and he didn't hide his feelings as he looked at her straight on. "How about it, Holly?"

After a second of silence she sighed. "I'll try, Brady. But come Monday morning…"

"Since I check out Sunday afternoon, okay."

He let out a relieved breath. He could go now, find Todd and Jeff, who were someplace in the crowd. Instead he stayed right where he was. "Alix is a charmer, a real girlie girl."

"Don't I know it. I had to force her to wear pants tonight instead of a dress." Holly smiled the way she used to in high school, a full-faced grin that crinkled the corners of her eyes.

Brady's heart stuttered in his chest. He wanted to see that smile again, even if it was almost too dark to appreciate it. "So that's how it all starts. Someday…" He shook his head and grinned. "Watch out, boys."

This time she laughed. "Not if I can help it."

He hadn't heard that sound in years. His own grin widened. Any minute now, the first firework would explode over the lake, and it was time to meet up with his buddies. "It's too dark to find Todd and Jeff. Is it okay if I watch the fireworks with you?"

He hadn't meant to ask, half hoped she'd say no. And wished he could see her eyes.

"I suppose," she said as she sat down on the edge of the blanket.

Brady knew where Todd's car was. He'd meet his buds there after the show. "Will Alix mind?"

"No. You were good with her."

"Was I?" Careful to keep his distance, he sat down on the opposite side of the blanket. "I don't have much experience with kids."

"You like them, though. That's obvious." She wrapped her arms around her knees and angled her head, her expression lost in shadow. "I'm surprised you don't have any of your own."

"I wouldn't mind a kid or two, but first I'd need to get married again. Something I don't see happening."

"Why not?"

"Once was enough."

"Was it that bad?"

"Worse." Jan had married him for his status as a football pro, nothing more. But he wasn't interested in hashing over old business. "What about you, Holly? If you don't mind my asking, what happened to Alix's father? All I know is what I heard at the last reunion, that he was a pro skier and out of the picture. Was he married or something?"

"I'd never get involved with a married man," she chided, sounding insulted. "Vince was here on vacation, staying at the lodge. We didn't know each other long enough to fall in love. By the time I discovered I was pregnant he was in Austria, skiing. He thought I should have an abortion, but I just couldn't. He paid my medical bills, and that was that."

"No child support?" The guy sounded like a first-class jerk to Brady.

Holly shook her head. "I didn't ask for it. I didn't want him barging into our lives later and demanding his rights. We signed a binding agreement stating that he waived his parental rights, and in return I waived my rights to support payments."

"His loss. That's some kid he's missing out on."

"Thank you."

Her pleased tone warmed him. Damned if he didn't want to put his arm around her and pull her close. But there were hundreds of people around, including her mother and daughter.

Besides, underneath the pleasantries she was mad at him. And she wanted a husband. No, cozying up to Holly was a bad idea.

Alix and Holly's mother came back. If Mrs. Stevens was surprised to find Brady sitting on the blanket, she didn't act it. She glanced from Holly to Brady and beamed. He pretended not to notice.

Holly did the same, her gaze on Alix. "Did you have fun, sweetie?"

"Uh-huh. Nana let me do two sparklers at once!" The little girl flopped onto the blanket beside her mother. "Hi, Mr. Cornell. The fireworks are about to start," she said as if his being there was natural.

At the moment, it did feel good. Brady hoped the warmth between him and Holly lasted through the weekend.

After that it was back to reality.

Chapter Three

As the fireworks wound down, Brady glanced at Holly. She was shooting tender looks at Alix, who had stretched out and fallen asleep sometime during the display. She was crazy about her daughter. Well, she was a neat kid.

Relaxing on the blanket, not close enough to touch but close enough to fuel some hot fantasies, was great. Brady couldn't help thinking what his life would have been like if he and Holly had stayed together and Alix was theirs. But they'd broken up a week before the senior prom. Since then they rarely saw each other.

Now his company was about to take away her livelihood. Brady felt rotten about that. He wished he could figure out a way to change things, but he was a pawn in TYR's frenzy to add hotels to their fast-growing chain. The endless acquisitions game was getting old and he was tired of feeling like pond scum. It'd be good to move up the ladder and be next in line as CEO, a position where he could work on changing the corporate policy of closing the shops that hotels often housed and laying off employees.

When the spectacular display ended, Holly looked his way and brushed her hands together, as if she was finished with the chore of acting nice. He didn't blame her, but he hoped she'd honor their agreement and stay civil through the weekend.

"Best fireworks I've seen since I lived here," he said.

"Spectacular." Her mother yawned. "We enjoyed having you with us, Brady. You're welcome anytime."

"Thanks, Mrs. Stevens."

Holly began to pack their things into a bag. "You'd better go find Todd and Jeff," she said, her attention on the bag.

"Holly!" her mother said. "Don't be rude."

Thank you, Mrs. Stevens. "Yeah, Holly. You need me to carry Alix to your car. Then I'll meet my friends."

"I wasn't being rude." Holly raised her head defensively. "I don't want to keep you from your friends is all. Alix is heavy, but if you want to carry her, that'd be great. Then I won't have to wake her up and make her walk."

Brady lifted the little girl, then pushed to his feet. Holly was mistaken—Alex wasn't heavy. Even in a dead sleep she weighed next to nothing. "Where's your car?"

Holly shook out the blanket. "The row farthest away from the road, I'm afraid," she replied as she and her mother folded and stuffed it into a second bag.

"No problem. Todd's car isn't far from there."

As they made their way over the trampled meadow-grass, men, women and children passed them, some talking in low voices, others laughing, others silent and sleepy.

Alix mumbled and snuggled against Brady's chest. Strands of her hair tickled under his chin. His chest expanded with feeling. Was this what his friend Mickey meant about kids making a man feel protective and soft at the same time?

"It's a long drive back," Mrs. Stevens said. "I'd better visit the Porta-Potty. I'll meet you at the car."

"I really appreciate this," Holly said as she and Brady reached the car. She unlocked the back door.

While Brady gently placed Alix on the seat, Holly stowed the bags in the trunk. Then she buckled in her daughter, straightened and closed the door.

"Thanks again, Brady, from both Alix and me."

"My pleasure." The urge to kiss Holly grabbed him. He touched her cheek. "I enjoyed myself tonight."

Though it was dark in the makeshift parking area, headlights of departing cars lit her face. Her expression was open and warm. "Me, too."

She tipped up her chin a fraction and he knew she'd let him kiss her, even if she was mad at him. But the night was full of nosy eyes, and her mom would be back soon…. He leaned down and brushed her lips, nothing hot, just a friendly good-night kiss.

The brief taste was as sweet as he remembered and not nearly enough. Brady didn't dare risk more. Not here. Not now. He gazed into her eyes. "Why did we break up?"

"Don't you remember? You wanted sex. I did, too, but not unless we were engaged. And here we are."

"Oh, I remember the sex part." They'd come close to making love more than a few times, but Holly had refused to go all the way without a ring on her finger. At eighteen, with a football scholarship to college, he hadn't been ready for marriage—no matter how hot he was for Holly.

Brady still wanted her. Badly. Even after all the women he'd been with and the years that had passed, making love with Holly was a fantasy that stayed with him. "At least you came to your senses about that," he said. "How long did it take?"

"Not long. A few months into my freshman year of college. If you'd just been patient…"

But patience never had been Brady's strength. And sex with Holly was out. She was and always would be the woman he couldn't have, the one he fantasized over, period.

Wielding a battery-powered lantern, Jeff and Todd ambled toward him.

"Figured we'd find you sooner or later," Jeff said, holding up the light. "You need a ride back, or are you going home with Holly?"

Home with Holly. Despite himself, Brady liked the sound of that.

Holly didn't. Her mouth tightened. "Brady's going with *you*."

Yep, nothing but fantasies for him. "See you later, Holly. Tell your mom I said good night."

"I will. 'Night, Brady."

She opened the door on the driver's side and slid in.

FRIDAY NIGHT Holly stood in the bathroom off the Silver Cliff Lodge's lobby, staring at her reflection. Thanks to the skillful cut, her blond-tinted hair swung nicely just above her shoulders. With a rhinestone necklace and earrings, a glittery shawl and a sparkly belt, the black shift she'd worn all day had been transformed to a cocktail dress. Sheer stockings and strappy, three-inch sandals finished off the outfit.

Not bad for a woman who had spent a full day at work. A woman soon to be out of a job. Her stomach knotted with worry. But no, she wasn't going there this weekend. From now through Sunday she would push her troubles aside and enjoy herself.

These days she didn't get out much at night, and the chance to spend an entire evening with adults…well, it was going to be fun. "Fun, Holly," she told her reflection. "Got that?"

She was glad her mom had agreed to watch Alix during the mixer tonight and the dance tomorrow night. She forced a smile. That was better.

Now for the lipstick. She pursed her mouth and thought about the brief brush of Brady's lips on hers. The sweetness had stayed with her a long time last night. It had only been a little kiss, nothing like the deep, passionate ones they'd shared in high school, but potent all the same. So powerful, she'd even daydreamed about it once or twice today.

Once or twice? Make that a whole lot. Holly frowned. She'd agreed to be civil, not waste time fantasizing about the man.

She spun away from the mirror and fiddled with the Class of '93 button and the name badge given when she'd registered for the reunion. Not wanting a pinhole in her dress, she attached both to the strap of her handbag.

"I will have fun tonight," she stated in a loud voice that echoed off the walls. Ready at last, she exited the bathroom and headed for the dining room.

Wearing a bright smile, she moved down the hallway, barely noting the worn flowered carpet or the dingy walls.

Every restaurant in town was booked for various reunion-class parties, and the dining room, which wasn't quite as shabby as the rest of the lodge, was packed with alumni, who were talking, eating and drinking. The crowd and noise were overpowering. At five foot five in heels, Holly couldn't see over the people, but somewhere in the room, Aileen and Bill and others from their class—she wouldn't let herself think about Brady—had snagged a table. At least that was the plan. What she needed was a margarita and something to eat.

Minutes later, drink and a plate of hors d'oeuvres in hand, she made her way leisurely through the crowd, stopping to greet and chat with people from other graduating classes. By the time she spotted Aileen and Bill at a long table near the window, her feet were starting to hurt and she was ready to sit down.

Aileen waved her over to the seat she'd saved near one end. To Holly's relief and disappointment, Brady was not at the table. *Fun,* she reminded herself. *I will have fun.*

"Good to see you, Holly." "You look beautiful," locals and classmates from out of town, some arriving only hours ago, said as she sat down.

Many of them had noticed Brady sharing her blanket last night, but thankfully not one person mentioned that fact. Most knew about the pending TYR sale. She was leaning toward the head of the table, chatting with Charlie Parks, an up-and-

coming playwright who had arrived with his wife this afternoon, all the way from London, when Aileen elbowed her.

"Here comes Brady."

Holly had filled her in on their agreement to be nice to each
other the whole weekend. She hadn't shared her confusion or
mentioned the little kiss that kept teasing through her mind.

Aileen glanced at the opposite end of the table. "Look at
Monica Combs trying to get his attention." She narrowed her
eyes. "I don't like her. She's a vamp. Even if she is the Realtor
for Bill's project."

Holly didn't mind Monica, who was friendly with everyone,
especially men. What she didn't like was the way the woman
ogled Brady, as though she wanted to devour him.

"Brady, sit down here!" Aileen called out over the noise.
"There's a seat across from Holly."

Eyebrows raised, including Monica's, and Holly knew
people were curious and puzzled. They'd sat together at last
night's fireworks, yet his company was booting her out. Now
they'd sit together again. What was going on?

"They promised to treat each other decently all weekend,"
Carla Plummer explained from the other end of the table.

Carla and Holly weren't close, yet that she knew this tidbit
of information came as no surprise. In this town, people knew
everything about everyone.

Brady gave an aw-shucks shrug, and Holly offered a non-
chalant smile. Then she turned again to Charlie and his wife.
"You were talking about the theater in London?"

A waiter replenished the platters of crackers and cheese
along the table. For a while everyone nibbled, drank and
talked. Charlie and his wife told entertaining stories, but Holly
listened with an ear cocked toward Brady. He and Bill, who
hadn't had a chance to catch up until now, were talking.

Bill had asked about the lodge, but Brady had changed the
subject to tomorrow morning's dedication, the kickoff of the high

school's transformation into condo units. The mayor had set the date of the dedication so that visiting alumni could take part.

"Construction starts next week," Bill said. "Keeping the building's historical integrity has been an architectural challenge, but I think we've done it. The units will be nice."

"Nice?" Aileen gaped at him. "Gorgeous is more like it, and quite a good investment. Do you realize that several units already are presold? People plan to live in them part of the year and rent them the rest. With skiing in the winter and hiking in the summer, tourism has become a growing year-round business, so why not? There's plenty of opportunity for everyone."

"No kidding." Now even Charlie was listening. He glanced at his wife. "We may want to look into one of the condos. Who's handling the sales?"

"I am," Monica said, waving a hand. "I'll pass you my card."

While the business card moved from hand to hand and people talked excitedly about the growing tourist trade, Holly thought about the depressing fact that she, Alix and her mother were losing out. Somehow she had to find a new location for the shop and figure out how to pay for the move and the higher rent.

"I'm sorry, Holly," Aileen murmured, biting her lip. "I didn't mean to bring you down with all this talk about business." She glanced at Brady. "This must be awkward for you, too."

He nodded solemnly, his expression so guilt-ridden that Holly almost felt sorry for him.

"But Holly and I aren't going there—at least, not this weekend." He cast her an anxious look. "Are we?"

"No," she said firmly. "This weekend is for having fun, period."

She sounded so certain that she almost believed herself.

Chapter Four

The jangle of the phone woke Brady from a dreamless sleep. Cracking open one eye, he groped for the phone. It wasn't on the left side of the bed. What the—Oh, yeah, he wasn't at home. He was at the lodge.

Rolling over, he grabbed the receiver. "Brady here."

"You were supposed to report in," Hal Waters, Brady's boss, said in his usual no-nonsense tone.

At seven on Saturday morning? Brady groaned. "Don't you ever relax? We've only just recovered from a national holiday, and you know I'm tied up with my reunion this weekend." He sat up, then swung his legs over the edge of the bed.

"Since when did you take off weekends?"

"Since now. Got a problem with that?"

"I do when you're in the middle of negotiations."

Brady thought about Holly and the other hotel employees he'd met so far. Knowing his company soon would put them on the street felt rotten, and he'd tossed and turned for hours. "I'm not sure this is the right hotel for us," he said.

"What was that? Because I know I didn't hear what I think I heard."

"The lodge needs more work than we realized," he said, glancing at the worn carpet and peeling wallpaper. "The bathrooms are old and the rooms and lobby need extensive renovations. It'll cost way too much for our budget."

"So we'll lower our offer. Webb is so eager to sell and retire he'll take anything. You're the best, Brady. You can talk him into it. That's why you're in line for CEO."

He would dangle that carrot. "I don't think we should buy it," Brady repeated. "I don't like putting people I know out of work."

"If you don't care about the promotion, say it now. Because I can bring in Thoreen to handle the deal."

Carl Thoreen was a weaselly little man Brady detested. "Keep him out of this." Brady scrubbed a hand over his face. "I'll handle the negotiations."

"That's what I wanted to hear. If you're hell-bent to party this weekend, go ahead. But keep your distance from those people so you can do your job. Your future depends on it." The phone clicked.

Brady hung up, wondering whether it wasn't time to find new employment. At that rebel thought, he scowled and stalked to his suitcase. For years he'd worked long hours, day in and day out, all for this promotion. Nothing was getting in his way, including his conscience.

Now he had a dedication to go to, and two days to enjoy himself. Come Monday, he would put together the sales plan TYR expected, using estimates of needed repairs to justify the rock-bottom offer.

By the time Holly, her mom and Alix arrived at Silver Cliff High for the dedication Saturday morning, a crowd had gathered.

The weather was perfect—sunny and warm but not yet hot. Brady was somewhere in the crowd—Holly sensed it. Wearing a happy face last night hadn't been easy, and she was in no mood to see him today or at tonight's gala dinner and reunion dance. Avoiding him wasn't possible, but she could try.

Holding Alix's hand, she moved to just in front of the high

school's wide front steps, where her view was limited to the mayor and the people to either side. Unusually silent, her mother followed along.

While Alix was dressing this morning, Holly had told her mother about the agreement she and Brady had made to be civil through the weekend. "That's the only reason we're speaking to each other," she'd explained.

She hadn't mentioned her unnerving attraction to Brady, but the glimmer in her mother's eyes made her wonder whether she'd guessed. Thankfully she hadn't said another word about him.

Now her mother frowned. "I feel silly coming to the dedication ceremony. I didn't even graduate from Silver Cliff High School, and I certainly don't care about the condos."

"Daddy and I did, so you're invited by proxy."

As her mother and Alix chatted with friends and everyone waited for Mayor Passky to start the dedication, Holly tried to fill her mind with happy thoughts. Yet she couldn't help worrying about her future. How was she going to support Alix?

That was nerve-racking enough. Even more upsetting were her feelings for Brady. She was strongly attracted to him. Which was confusing and bad. Very bad. Brady was all wrong for her.

Suddenly people moved aside as Mayor Passky, an alum from the Class of '80, shook hands on his way to the steps. Standing a few feet from the old wooden front door, he tapped the microphone someone had set up. A hush fell over the group.

"As you all know, Silver Cliff High has closed its doors forever," he said in the deep, beautiful voice that had made him a popular disc jockey before he'd turned to politics. "When the building reopens, it will house twenty-four condominiums and have a new name, Mountain View Estates. For those who may not have heard, Mountain View High, the brand-new, state-of-the-art high school for Silver Cliff and other nearby communities, will open its doors in August."

Who'd have thought closing the high school would make a girl cry? Sniffling and swiping her eyes, Holly glanced at the glorious Rocky Mountains rimming the horizon.

"For those alumni here today, please join me tonight at the Silver Palace for a gala dinner, followed by an all-alumni dance in the high-school gym. I don't want to give away any secrets, but my lovely wife, Bonnie, Class of '82—" he nodded at a slim, attractive brunette who waved her hand in the air "—and her committee have worked hard to make Silver Cliff High School's final dance an unforgettable evening." He scanned the crowd. "There's former pro quarterback Brady Cornell." He pointed at Brady, somewhere in the middle of the crowd, then led the applause.

Surrounded by people, Holly couldn't see him. She imagined him waving and flashing an irresistible grin.

"Tragically, Brady's career was cut short by a knee injury," the mayor continued, "but we know he got his start right here. For Brady and the other athletes here today, please join me in one last hurrah for our beloved Soaring Eagle mascot and team. Go, Soaring Eagles!"

He pumped his fist high, and the air rumbled with enthusiastic voices. Over the crowd, Holly was sure she heard Brady.

"Mama, I feel sick," Alix said.

She did look pale. "Oh, dear. We'd better go home. Come on, Mother."

Intent on getting Alix to the car, she kept her head down and didn't stop to chat with anyone.

Just before Alix climbed into the car, she threw up.

SHORTLY AFTER the dance started Saturday night, Holly pulled in to the paved parking lot behind the high school. Thanks to Alix's nasty flu bug, she'd missed the dinner at the Silver

Palace Hotel, a beautiful building with a brand-new conference center that held a thousand people. The Palace was newer and much nicer than the Silver Cliff Lodge, was always busy with conventions and tourists. Their thriving gift shop was every bit as nice as Holly's and she and the owner enjoyed a friendly rivalry that would soon end.

But Holly didn't want to think about that now. She didn't want to think about how exhausted she was, either. Caring for a sick child was demanding and wearing. If this wasn't the last-ever reunion at the high school, she'd have crawled into bed right after Alix. Instead, with her mother urging her on, she was here. She'd have a good time, too, or die trying.

Nearly every parking slot was taken, but she found a space at the very back of the lot. For several moments she sat in the car, unable to see beyond the halogen lights around the perimeter of the lot.

Her stomach felt as if a giant hand were squeezing it and her hands were ice-cold. Was this the beginning of Alix's flu bug? No, she didn't feel sick. More…nervous. For some reason, coming here by herself was hard, much harder than the ten-year reunion.

Ridiculous. This was an alumni gathering, a time to visit with friends. No one cared that she was alone. Brady would be, too. Holly frowned. When she saw him tonight, she'd continue to be civil. But mostly she'd stay away from him.

She exited the car and made her way to the gym around the side of the school, the heels of her glittery silver mules tapping smartly on the pavement. The crisp, clear night invigorated her, and by the time she reached the battered metal gym doors she felt better. Holly adjusted her name badge and Class of '93 button, smoothed down the tomato-red cocktail dress—bought on sale—and walked inside.

A wide hall separated the gym from the exit, but through the closed gym doors voices and an eighties rock 'n' roll song floated toward her. Humming to the music, she headed for the rectangular table, where her beloved English teacher, Miss Blanchard, sat to sign people in.

"Hello, Miss Blanchard," she said over the loud music.

"Hello, Holly." The older woman's plump, ageless face lit in a fond smile. "You look lovely tonight. How's Alix?"

Naturally she'd know about Alix. "Better. She was sleeping when I left tonight. Aren't you coming inside, to the dance?"

"Someone needs to stay out here and check off people. I'll be in later."

"That this is our last time ever in this school feels sad," Holly said.

"It certainly does. I taught here for thirty-three years. But we'll have photos and our memories, and the building will still be here," Miss Blanchard said. "It'll just be different."

Holly liked her positive view of the situation. "I wonder where we'll hold our future reunions?" she asked.

"The Silver Palace, or the lodge—or should I say, TYR. What are you going to do with your gift shop?"

"I don't know yet." Fresh worry weighted Holly's shoulders, but she didn't want to think about that now. She didn't want to think about Brady, either, but knowing he was inside or soon would be, she couldn't help herself.

"Holly, are you all right?" Miss Blanchard asked, squinting through her rimless glasses.

In high school, Holly had confided more than once to the nurturing teacher, who was great at helping teens solve their problems. But she was no longer a schoolgirl, and this was not the time.

"Alix's flu wore me out, but I'll be fine." She forced a smile. "Guess I'll go inside the gym now. See you later."

The gym looked wonderful, decorated with photos of the school and classes through the years. Overhead a glitter ball swirled slowly, showering the scarred wooden floor and tables around the periphery with shards of bright light. Just as it had at most of the high-school dances. But there were teachers dancing instead of chaperoning, and the swing music playing was from before Holly's time.

"I feel like I've stepped into a time warp," she murmured.

"I know what you mean," said a seventy-something woman. "Except in my day, we didn't have those mirror balls."

Her husband flashed teeth too white to be real. "We're the Jamiesons, Barton and Nell. Nell is from the Class of '48."

Nell smiled, her gray eyes warm behind her trifocals. "I haven't missed a single reunion yet, and when I heard about Silver Cliff High closing forever…" She shook her head. "We came all the way from Sarasota for this."

"Wow," Holly said. "I'm Holly Stevens, Class of '93, and I live right here in town. Welcome. Were you at the dinner tonight?"

"Yes, and it was lovely," Nell said. "What a beautiful facility."

"Isn't it?" Holly said as Mayor Passky, who in honor of the evening had slipped into his DJ persona, played a new tune.

"This toe-tappin' Mills Brothers music makes me feel eighteen again." Barton grasped Nell's hand. "May I have this dance?"

"You may. Nice to meet you," Nell called out as he led her to the dance floor.

In no time they were swallowed up in the crowd.

At the side of the stage a group of women Holly knew, but not from her class, were dancing together. They gestured her over, but she didn't feel like dancing just yet. She hoped to find Aileen and hear about the dinner she'd missed. She glanced at the tables around the room, which were filled with people of all ages. Some faces were familiar; others she didn't recognize.

What to do now? Hardly aware of her actions, she searched the room for Brady.

She found him, surrounded by men and women, including Milton Mahoney, Silver Cliff's beak-nosed principal for the past thirty years. In a dark suit, dress shirt and tie, Brady looked so handsome…. Holly released a dreamy sigh. He had no business looking that good. He said something and everyone around him laughed. Some of the women eyed him with more than casual interest.

She prickled at that. How dare they? Then she caught herself. Brady was single and available. If he wanted one of those women, she certainly didn't care.

Turning her back on Brady and his adoring fan club, she followed an arrow that pointed to the refreshment table, which, because there was no room in the gym, stood in a hallway adjacent to it. Since most everyone here had eaten at the Silver Palace, the area was almost deserted. And, once the door shut behind her, far quieter.

Only a few lonely hearts here, no one she knew. Two well-stocked tables held beer, wine, soda and punch, and a host of finger foods. As Holly pondered her choices and introduced herself to several people, the music stopped.

Through the closed doors she heard the mic squeak. "Welcome to Sliver Cliff High's all-years reunion," the mayor said in his rich voice. "I'm Mike Passky, mayor of this fine town, proud class of '80 graduate and your DJ for tonight."

While he paused for cheers and whoops, Holly finished a canapé, then wiped her hands on a napkin. Everyone else headed for the gym door.

"You may be wondering why you've been listening to music from decades ago," the mayor said. "Several of the alumni here tonight graduated as early as 1940. I'll be playing popular music from the past sixty-seven years." Applause again broke out. "At this morning's dedication I promised you a surprise or two tonight and—"

Afraid of missing something, Holly followed the others into the gym.

Chapter Five

Mayor Passky was long-winded, Brady decided, but he did have a smooth voice that was easy to listen to, especially with a few beers under your belt. Not wanting to block anyone's view, he was at the back of the room, near the cinder-block wall plastered with old black-and-white photos of the school and school events.

"To share those surprises, I'd like to introduce my lovely wife, Bonnie, Class of '82."

The crowd, buoyed by drinks and good food from the dinner at the Silver Palace, cheered again.

For a woman in her mid forties, Bonnie Passky looked good. As she walked up the four steps to the podium, her blue silk dress swished.

The doors at the side of the room opened, drawing his attention. Several people Brady didn't know walked in, but his gaze homed in on Holly. He barely heard Bonnie. He'd heard about Alix's flu, and had missed Holly at dinner.

She didn't notice him, but he had no doubt that when she did, she'd walk the other way. Probably for the best. Last night's party had been awkward, and he wasn't interested in a repeat.

That didn't mean he couldn't look. He'd always liked her in red, and this dress, short and snug, with thin little straps, showed off her soft curves and great legs.

"We're going to start off with a rousing welcome for the

people from the Class of 1940," Bonnie said. "Would you please acknowledge yourselves?"

From a table along the side two elderly women smiled and waved. At that ripe age and having traveled a long way to get here, they deserved applause. Brady clapped, along with everyone else.

The mayor delivered framed photographs of the school to each woman. Next, awards were given for who had traveled the farthest. Charlie Parks won that one.

"Now for an acknowledgment to tradition," Bonnie said. "As you all may recall, each year during senior prom, our school chooses a king and queen. This tradition started in the 1930s. I know there is 'royalty' here tonight. When I call your name, if you're here, please come up."

The last thing Brady wanted was to stand on the stage with Holly. He noted the dismay on her face and her longing glance at the exit. As if she felt his gaze, she finally saw him. He gave a helpless shrug and she returned it.

Bonnie was up to the Class of '92 now. When she called Brady and Holly, they joined some forty couples, many of whom hadn't seen each other in decades, on the stage.

"I feel so self-conscious," Holly whispered.

"It'll be over in a minute," Brady assured her in an equally low voice.

Only, it wasn't. After polite applause, Bonnie ordered the floor cleared and sent the couples onto the floor to dance. Nothing to do but get this over with.

Brady held out his arms. Looking ill at ease, Holly walked into them. Even in heels she only reached his shoulder.

"You smell good," he said, sniffing her hair.

"Thank you."

She felt small in his arms. And stiff, very stiff.

"It's only one dance, Holly. Relax," he said, careful not to hold her too tight.

"You're right. Okay." She blew out a breath and let him pull her closer.

"That's better. How's Alix?"

"Over the worst of it, thanks." She seemed more relaxed now. "Dr. Jacobs said it was a twenty-four-hour thing."

"Glad to hear that." He tightened his arms.

Despite their difference in height she fit perfectly against him. They hadn't made out for fourteen-plus years, but hot images flooded his head. He'd never seen her naked, but it wasn't hard to picture her that way, her thighs gripping his hips…

His body stirred. Stifling a groan, he eased back a fraction.

Then he noted Bill, Aileen, a slew of other people watching them with interest. Brady scowled. "Everyone is watching us."

"That's what people do when the prom king and queen dance," Holly said. "Don't you remember?"

"How could I forget? We broke up a week before the prom, but my dad made me bring you anyway. He said a Cornell doesn't back away from an obligation."

"My mother said almost the same thing. Except, she hoped we'd make up."

Though that hadn't happened, they'd danced this same way that night.

The song ended. Brady wasn't ready to let her go, but he didn't have much choice. The couples who hadn't come together broke apart and returned to their spouses or friends.

"That wasn't so bad," he said.

"No."

Neither of them moved.

Mayor Passky again took the mic. "That's all the surprises for now. As they said in that wonderful movie, shall we dance?"

A George Michael song from the early nineties filled the

air, a song Brady and Holly had once made out to at the boarded-up Pecos Silver Mine, where kids went to fool around. With the music and the memories he couldn't let her go, not yet.

"How about another dance?" he said, snagging her hand.

AS THE BEACH BOYS' song trailed off, Holly swiped her forehead, which was damp with sweat, and grinned at Brady. "I haven't danced like this in a long time."

She couldn't seem to stop smiling. Having fun was her goal and at the moment she definitely was. Still, she wondered at herself. Dancing to song after song with Brady, losing herself in his eyes, wanting him and knowing he wanted her, too. Was she out of her mind?

Around her and Brady, Aileen, Bill, Monica, who had paired up with an out-of-town alumnus named Bud, and several of their former friends and classmates laughed, mopped their brows and caught their breaths.

At least with so many people around, Holly wouldn't dare do something foolish like throw her arms around Brady and kiss him.

Secure in the knowledge that there truly was safety in numbers, she forgot everything but enjoying herself. Finally the music stopped. Hot and thirsty, she, Brady and most of the others headed for the refreshment table.

"Is this punch spiked?" she asked after draining two glasses. It hadn't tasted that way, but her brain felt muzzy. Or maybe dancing with Brady had clouded her mind.

"Probably."

His gaze combed over her, spreading heat that was difficult to ignore. She couldn't breathe for wanting him.

"Anybody up for taking a walk around the football field one last time?" Mickey Rennant asked.

"I am… Sure… Great idea," most of the group replied.

"Count me in," Brady said.

Given Holly's strong attraction to him, she couldn't go. Too dangerous. "I'll stay here," she said.

"Come on, Holly, it'll be fun," Brady coaxed, his eyes on hers. "A walk down memory lane."

That was the last thing Holly needed. But with Brady's big-eyed, puppy-dog face, how could she refuse? *Safety in numbers,* she reminded herself. *I'll be fine.*

She and Brady were the first out the door. Someone turned on the stadium lights, drowning out the stars and moon. Good. Who needed the romance? The air was cool, but Holly was warm, both from dancing and from walking beside Brady.

For a moment, standing on the field, everyone was silent.

"This may sound sappy, but even though I haven't played here since high school, I'm going to miss this old place," Brady said.

Murmurs of assent filled the air. Still leading the others, Holly and Brady cut across the field and ambled toward the bleachers.

Gradually the voices behind them faded away. Then she and Brady were alone. That wasn't safe. Squinting in the artificial light, she searched the field. "Where did everybody go? We should catch up."

"We'll find them later." Brady smiled at her. "Tonight has been fun, Holly. Like old times, only better."

The warmth in his eyes matched the feelings in her brimming heart. Memories flooded her. Laughing with Brady, sharing passionate kisses and more, aching to make love with him. And always pulling back, just in time.

Now she wished she *had* made love with him back in high school. At least she'd have gotten him out of her system and probably wouldn't feel so hot and bothered now. At the moment the urge to fall into his arms and let things go where they may was almost too strong to fight.

But sexual desire was only partly responsible for the emotion bubbling inside her. Truth was, she was still a little in love with Brady. Which was crazy and scary to boot. She glanced away. "It *has* been fun, but on Monday we won't be on speaking terms," she said, to remind both of them.

"Does it have to be that way? This is my job, Holly. Once the sale goes through, I'll get a big promotion."

"Is that why you won't try to stop the sale—for a promotion?" Anger blazed through her, and she latched on to it like a lifeline. Better to be mad than to desire him. She crossed her arms. "I should've guessed."

Brady swore. "With or without me, this sale is going through. I could disappear tomorrow and it'd still happen. And I'll say this again—without the sale the lodge will close. That'd put the whole staff out of work." His mouth tightened. "So quit blaming me for something I can't control."

He was right. As quickly as the anger had flared, it died. "I don't, not really. I'm sorry."

And she ought to go home. She pivoted toward the gym.

"Where are you going?"

"Back inside. We shouldn't be out here together."

"Sure we should. Our deal lasts through midnight tomorrow, remember?"

"If you mean being civil toward each other, I think we just broke that agreement."

"I accept your apology, Holly, and I hope you accept mine. You have the right to be angry. I shouldn't have lost my temper." He searched her face. "This is my last walk around the football field. I'd like to share it with you." He held out his hand.

She could no more refuse him than she could stop breathing. His warm grip all but swallowed her hand, and as they wandered silently toward the bleachers, her heart swelled with feeling, and memories again crowded her head.

"I must have watched dozens of football practices up there, and every home game." And she'd never even liked football. She'd been that wild for Brady.

No man had ever filled her heart and touched her soul as he had. Was it any wonder she still had feelings for him?

He grinned. "I used to grandstand quite a bit to impress you. Do you remember the first time I kissed you, after we won our first game junior year?"

How could she forget? She nodded. "You pulled me behind the bleachers where nobody could see. I was in awe that the school's youngest-ever varsity quarterback wanted to kiss me."

"You were the cutest girl around. I couldn't help myself," he said, smiling into her eyes.

Heat sizzled between them, and his grin faded. "You're no cute girl anymore."

"Oh," she said, disappointed. "That happens to every female. It's called getting old."

"That's not what I meant. You grew up and turned into a beautiful woman." He touched her cheek. "So very beautiful."

The words and his tender touch warmed her. And filled her with trepidation. She swallowed. "What are you saying, Brady?"

"That maybe I should kiss you behind the bleachers again."

His thumb stroked her cheek, and every nerve in her body came alive. For a whole lot more than a kiss. Right or wrong, tonight she would not refuse.

Holly lifted her face. "Maybe you should."

HOLLY'S LIPS were soft and warm. Holding her felt so good. Brady pulled her closer. She made a little sound in her throat and twined her arms around his neck, and the past flooded back as though everything had just happened yesterday. Her round breasts pressed against his chest and her hips tantalized his groin. Blood roared through his head.

He wanted her.

He deepened the kiss. Her lips parted, and he plunged his tongue into the slick warmth of her mouth. His body tightened and hardened. He molded his hands to her sweet behind, pushing her against his need. Holly met each kiss eagerly, which turned him on even more.

If he didn't touch her, he'd go mad. He slid the straps of her dress off her shoulders. His fingers skimmed the edge of her low-cut top, teasing and seductive. She caught her breath and leaned back a fraction. With hands that shook he slipped his palm inside the top and down her bra.

Her nipples were taut and swollen. She'd always been supersensitive. Growling with pleasure, Brady kept his touch light and teasing, the way he remembered she liked.

Her breathy moan drove him closer to the edge. But this wasn't the time or the place. He had no protection on him. Besides, as badly as he wanted Holly and she seemed to want him, making love wasn't a good idea.

"Holly," he panted, removing his hand and letting her go.

"What?" She sounded dazed.

"We shouldn't be doing this."

NEVER HAD HOLLY desired a man so much. Tangled up with her need was the realization that, want to or not, she'd never stopped loving Brady. Since he wasn't about to get married again and she probably wouldn't see him alone after tonight, this was her only chance to make love with him. She wasn't the one-night-stand type, but for Brady she was willing to make an exception.

If she didn't, she thought she might die. "I don't care, Brady. I want to make love. Just this once, for old times' sake." A memory to cherish forever.

"There was no old times' sake, remember?"

"That's why I want to make love with you tonight. We both wonder what it'll be like together. Let's find out." She cupped his face and searched his gaze so he'd believe her. "Please, Brady, make love with me."

After a long moment he blew out a breath. "All right, but not here. Let's go to the lodge. We can get to the parking lot without going back inside."

With both of them leaving at the same time, people would no doubt notice and talk, but Holly didn't care. She nodded. "I'll follow you there."

TWENTY MINUTES LATER Holly stood in Brady's room, amazed at herself. Not even the drive to the lodge with the windows down and cold air blowing in her face had changed her mind.

She was about to make love with a man who didn't want marriage and who was orchestrating the sale of the lodge. If she was smart, she'd drive straight home and lock herself in the house. But she simply could not.

Brady shut the drapes and flipped on the lamp on one side of the bed. Then turned toward her, his eyes dark and probing. "Are you sure about this?"

Trembling from nerves or anticipation or both, she attempted to smile. "I'm a little nervous."

"Truth be told, so am I. I've dreamed about this for over fourteen years," he said, his face intent as he moved toward her.

She bit her lip. "I hope I won't disappoint you."

"Not possible."

Grasping her face between his warm palms, he gazed into her eyes, and she forgot her fears. Eyelids lowering, he leaned down and kissed her, the gentle press of his lips promising a night to remember.

The heat that had simmered for days and had flared on the football field licked through her. Feverish and feeling like a starving woman, she wrapped her arms around his neck and urged him closer. Several long, passionate kisses later, Brady broke contact.

Breathing hard, he rested his forehead against hers. "Are we crazy for doing this?"

"Probably, but I don't care." Even so, she wasn't stupid. She stared into his liquid brown eyes. "I should have asked this earlier, but are you healthy?"

"Tested a few months ago and haven't been with anyone since. You?"

"I haven't been with a man since Holly's father. I'm clean. Do you have protection?"

"Always." He moved to the luggage stand and rifled through his suitcase. Grabbed a handful of condoms and set them on the bedside table.

"So you were planning to have sex while you were here? If not with me, then someone else?" To her own ears she sounded jealous, but she had to know.

"Not necessarily, but I like to be prepared."

"That's smart." She studied the low-pile carpet.

"Holly?" She could feel his gaze. "Have you changed your mind?"

Nervous or not, she wasn't about to back out now. She unzipped her dress and shimmied out of it. "Does that answer your question?"

"Sure does." His appreciative gaze moved from her black demi bra to her matching bikini panties to her thigh-highs. "You are so damn fine."

"I've had a child, Brady. I'm not."

"In my eyes, you are."

He tugged her close and kissed her. Again and again, until she was dizzy with the taste and smell of him. Somehow her bra disappeared, then her panties.

Brady studied her through hot, heavy-lidded eyes. "This—" one finger trailed a faded stretch mark on the side of her breast "—is beautiful."

Her nipples beaded in longing. The desire darkening his

face made her *feel* beautiful. And bold. She cupped her breasts and offered them to him.

A growl purled from his throat. He took one nipple in his mouth, then switched to the other, until she was squirming with need. When she was ready to collapse, he pulled back. Directed a hot look at her legs.

"Much as I like those stockings, they've got to go."

Kneeling at her feet, he peeled off each one with his skilled fingers. Then kissed the inside of her calf while she stood, clasping his solid shoulders for balance.

No one had ever removed her stockings or kissed her there. Tenderness and love and heat tumbled together inside her. He worked his way up her sensitive inner thigh, dangerously close to the part of her that most needed him. Moisture pooled between her legs. Her very shaky legs. "I can't stand up anymore," she said.

"Lean on me, babe." He lifted her in his arms and carried her to bed, the loving warmth on his face melting her. With one hand he tore off the bedspread before he gently laid her down. "Now, let me taste you."

He parted her thighs and started where he'd left off, his lips continuing a delicious path toward her center. At last he was there, opening her folds, licking and teasing until she was writhing with pleasure and tension. It had been a very long time since she'd been with a man and she did not want to climax alone.

She pushed him away. "Take off your clothes and love me."

Eyes locked on hers, he unbuttoned his shirt and tossed it aside, exposing a broad, muscled chest, a smattering of chest hair and a flat belly. Holly's gaze dropped to the strained zipper below.

"See what you do to me?" His expression dark and hungry and dangerous, he shed his dress slacks and kicked off his briefs.

He was big, and gloriously aroused. Holly swallowed. "You're the beautiful one."

"Oh, I have my flaws." He gestured at the long red scar on his knee, the injury that had cost him a career in pro football. "Does that hurt?"

"Now and then." Smirking, he glanced at his erection. "Right now another part of me hurts."

"Maybe I can make it feel better." Holly patted the bed beside her. "Come to Holly."

Feeling powerful and womanly, she pushed him onto his back. Brushed her thumb over his sensitive head. Caressed the thick, smooth shaft.

Brady groaned. "Enough."

He caught her wrist, then flipped her onto her back and covered her with his body. His skin against hers felt like heaven. His arousal nudged her sex. He kissed her and she lost herself in a haze of smells and tastes and desire.

Writhing under him, she moaned, "Please, Brady. I need you now."

He sheathed himself. And joined with her. Less than a heart-beat later she lost herself in a shattering climax.

When the tremors ended, Brady collapsed beside her. "That was really amazing."

"As good as you imagined?" she asked, languid against his side.

"Better." He kissed her forehead, his hand resting on her hip. "How was it for you?"

"Wonderful." *I love you, Brady.*

As badly as she longed to tell him, she bit back the words. He might like her. He might desire her. But he didn't want what she did—love and forever after.

Chapter Six

Brady awoke as Holly pulled out of his arms. He must have dozed off. Now he propped himself up on his elbow. "Where are you going?"

"My mother's watching Alix. I have to get home," she said, shielding herself with her dress while she collected her bra and panties from the floor.

His blood stirred. Did she even know how sexy she was? She was great in bed, too, and he wasn't ready to let her go. "I don't want you to go yet, babe. Can't you ask her to stay with Alix all night?"

"Better not." She ducked into the bathroom and returned dressed. "I wish…"

"What do you wish?"

"Nothing. I'll never forget tonight, Brady."

After the best sex of his life, neither would he. "It doesn't have to be over between us. We can still see each other. Denver isn't that far away."

"That won't work." She slid a comb from her purse and fixed her hair. "You're about to hammer out the details that will put me out of work." At his scowl she quickly added, "I know, I know, it's not your doing. But aside from the negotiations, I don't want to start something with you unless you're interested in marriage. And we both know you're not."

"But—"

"Shh." She held her finger to her lips, then stepped into her shoes. "Don't ruin this, Brady."

"Will you be at the brunch?"

She shook her head. "I'll be working. Goodbye."

She turned away, but not before he saw the tears in her eyes. He realized he'd hurt her, but it was too late for words or apologies. For she was gone.

"A SHAME YOU HAVE to miss the last reunion function for work," Holly's mother commented when she showed up to babysit Sunday morning.

"I really don't mind," Holly said. "I've already connected with everyone I wanted to see."

And then some. Making love with Brady had been beautiful and wonderful. And never would happen again. But she'd known that going in.

Brady would be at the brunch, and even if she hadn't had to work, the truth was, after last night, she didn't want to see him. Thank heavens he'd be leaving this afternoon, gone until business negotiations brought him back.

"At least you got to the dance."

Her mother's eyes were filled with questions, and Holly knew she wondered what had happened. Last night, pleading the late hour and fatigue, she'd staved off questions. She couldn't use that excuse now.

"It was great fun," she said. Eager to change the subject, she smiled at Alix, who had made a full recovery from the flu. "Would you like another piece of cheese toast, sweetie?"

"Yes, please."

"Did you dance with anyone special?" her mother inquired.

"Brady, if that's what you want to know. It was fun." She covered a slice of toast with cheese and popped it into the microwave to melt.

"Well, what happened?"

"Nothing! Now, please drop it."

"You're grouchy," Alix said.

Her mother raised her eyebrows and nodded.

"I didn't sleep well." After making love with Brady, how could she sleep?

"Did you have bad dreams?" Alix asked.

"You could say that." Her dreams had been full of Brady, dreams that never would come true. She sliced the cheese toast in half and dropped it onto Alix's plate, then kissed her forehead. "I'd better go or I'll be late. Be good for Nana."

"I hope you have a busy, profitable day," her mother said as Holly kissed her cheek.

"Me, too." She hurried out.

SUNDAY MORNING Brady was still hungry for Holly. Finding her stockings on the floor didn't help. They smelled of her light, flowery perfume. The whole damn room smelled of Holly. Of their lovemaking.

Leaning before the bathroom mirror, he lathered his face with shaving cream. Late last night he'd realized that after all these years, he still cared for her—a lot. If he weren't involved in the sale of the lodge, he wouldn't mind dating her and getting to know Alix better.

He dragged the razor over his chin. But he *was* involved with the sale in a major way. Holly was right. Seeing each other would only complicate matters. Especially since she wanted to get married and he didn't.

Stuff he knew but conveniently had forgotten last night. He nicked his jaw. Served him right.

He felt like a first-class jerk, and hated that he'd hurt her. She'd be at the gift shop later. He would stop in and apologize. That eased his guilty conscience.

But what to say? He finished shaving, then rinsed his face. A long run would cool his body and unfog his brain. Surely then he'd figure out what to say. Forget the brunch. He'd ha enough of those people. He dressed in his jogging clothes and headed out.

The bright sunlight, crisp morning air and grueling run did the trick and cleared his head. But he remained clueless about how to patch things up between Holly and him.

Back in his room, winded and sweaty, he ordered room service, then showered and dressed. By the time breakfast arrived, the gift shop was open. He ate quickly, then slipped Holly's stockings into his pocket and rode the elevator down.

Through the large window of her shop he saw her talking to an older couple, pointing to a black-and-white photograph of Silver Cliff that hung on the wall. Her face was interested and alive. Beautiful. Brady's chest filled with emotions he had no business feeling. He wanted her so much he ached.

Suddenly she glanced through the window and saw him. Her cheeks flushed before she returned her attention to the couple.

Brady waited for them to leave before he entered the shop.

"What are you doing here?" Holly asked. "Why aren't you at the brunch?"

He tucked her hair behind her ear, a little thing that shouldn't have aroused him. But everything about Holly turned him on. "I wanted to talk to you."

Expression carefully neutral, she backed up a step. "There's no need."

"About last night—I never meant to hurt you."

Her eyes went soft with forgiveness. "I'm a big girl, Brady. I'll get over it." She straightened an already neat stack of I heart Silver Cliff T-shirts. "When do you check out?"

"Soon." He reached into his pocket for the stockings. "You forgot these last night."

"I thought so. Thank you."

Holly accepted the stockings from him and shoved them under the counter. Two teenage girls sauntered in. She offered Brady a sad smile. "Well, goodbye again."

Chapter Seven

Brady drove to Denver on autopilot, his thoughts full of Holly. The way she looked at him, her smile. Her enthusiasm for her work and her love for Alix. The little sounds she made when she came apart in his arms, and the feel of her soft body snuggled beside him after.

Then in the gift shop… He'd expected… What? That she'd want more from him. Instead she'd let him off the hook. He should be grateful. So why did he feel hollow?

Back in the TYR headquarters he immersed himself in work but couldn't summon much enthusiasm. Truth was, he was in a foul temper. His boss, Hal Waters, didn't help matters.

"What the hell is wrong with you?" he said when Brady snarled at him. "Did some old high-school girlfriend get under your skin? I warned you to keep your distance. Pull yourself together, man, and get back on track."

Brady couldn't deny that he was way off track. He'd never felt like this about anyone, not even his ex-wife.

"Did you work up a cost sheet for Webb?" Hal asked.

"Yes, and in my opinion his asking price is fair as it stands," Brady said. He believed that, too.

"Forget your opinion. Lower the bid."

Brady shook his head. "I won't do that."

Hal leaned forward, his beefy face too close. "You'd better think carefully about that, Brady, and about your future here.

Because unless you negotiate the sale at our terms…" His eyes narrowed, and threatening, he strode out.

Brady did as his boss suggested, and thought about things. There was nothing different about his boss or TYR's method of operation. Brady had changed, though, and was beginning to wonder why he'd ever enjoyed working here.

He also wondered how he'd walked away from Holly, and how to get her back. Because he loved her. That didn't scare him the way it should have.

Thing was, she wanted a ring on her finger. Now, *that* scared him. His only experience with marriage had been unhappy and painful.

But aside from that, what about the sale and his promotion? What about Holly's shop and her friends who soon would be out of jobs? That always would come between them.

Instead of contacting Barton Webb to negotiate TYR's deal, he mulled over the questions for days. At the end of the week, torn and agonizing, he sat at a local restaurant for lunch, barely tasting his sandwich. If he were half as smart as TYR thought he was, he'd resign and start his own company. Buy the lodge himself at a fair price, with investors to help finance the deal.

Intrigued at the idea and also shaken by it, he mulled over the thought while he ate. Climbing to the top of the corporate ladder was what he'd worked for all these years. Was he willing to throw that away for Holly?

In the middle of a bite he spotted Hal striding toward him.

"There you are." Despite Brady's go-away scowl, his boss sat down. "You don't usually take off in the middle of the day. What did Webb say when you lowballed him?"

Brady set down his sandwich. "Can't this wait till after lunch?"

"I've waited long enough. Well?"

"I haven't talked to him."

Hal's jaw tightened. "I don't know what's eating you, Brady, and I don't care. Either you negotiate the sales price down today, or by God, I'll—"

"Fire me? Don't bother. I quit." Brady pushed back his chair.

Leaving Hal Waters gaping, he dropped a twenty on the table and walked away. He might feel lousy later, but at the moment he felt lighter than he had in years.

He couldn't wait to tell Holly. He couldn't wait to tell her he loved her. Sometime during the past few days he'd decided that marrying her was a risk worth taking. He would ask her to be his wife. He only hoped she said yes. And that Alix was okay with the idea. If not, he'd just work to win her over.

First things first, though. He'd line up financing and talk to Webb about selling to him at a fair price instead of accepting TYR's low offer. Exhilarated, amazed at himself and shaking his head, he began to empty his office.

BRADY HAD BEEN GONE two weeks now. Holly didn't expect to hear from him, and he didn't contact her. He didn't return to Silver Cliff, either. Instead Mr. Webb drove to Denver for meetings. He was closemouthed about the negotiations, but things seemed to be moving forward.

Holly spent what little spare time she had searching for retail space. Every lead ended in disappointment. It looked as if she'd be forced to close the gift shop for good. With a heavy heart she brushed up her résumé and searched the want ads.

And hoped for a miracle.

BY THE END OF July rumors were flying. People said the sale was off, that TYR had withdrawn and that Brady no longer worked for them. But Mr. Webb was in Denver, and there was no way to find out.

"Why don't you call Brady and ask him," Aileen suggested one afternoon when she stopped by the gift shop.

Holly had told her about everything, including their night together and her deep feelings for Brady. She angled her head. "You know I can't."

"Don't be silly. You're not calling to beg him to love you. You just want to know what's going on."

That made sense. "Okay, I'll do it later."

Aileen glanced around the empty shop. "What's wrong with right now?"

"A customer might wander in." And the thought of talking to Brady made her nervous. She needed time to screw up her courage.

"So? I can operate a cash register. Just go into the back room and do it."

As Holly sat down at the small desk in the back room, her heart pounded. Facing shelves of stock, she dialed directory assistance. "May I have the number of TYR in Denver?"

"I can give it to you."

She knew that voice. "Brady!" Disconnecting, she spun her chair around. He was as heart-stoppingly handsome as ever. Her heart lifted. "What are you doing here?"

"I hear you have questions about me."

"About the sale," she corrected. "I do."

"Fire away. Will you keep an eye on the shop, Aileen?" he called.

"No problem, Brady," she called back in a cheerful voice.

Brady closed the door separating the back room from the shop. "It's crowded in here."

"Yes, it is." Bursting with curiosity, Holly eyed him. "Why are you really here?"

"Couple of reasons. First, to share the good news. This morning Barton Webb accepted Cornell Associates' offer to buy the lodge."

"Cornell Associates?"

"The company I formed when I resigned from TYR. I own the controlling interest, and Charlie Parks and other people from Silver Cliff own the rest. You wouldn't believe how quickly the deal came together. The lodge is our first acquisition."

"You're buying the lodge?" Holly wasn't sure she understood. "Exactly what does that mean?"

"For starters, you get to keep your store. And your friends who own shops here and all the employees now employed will hold on to their jobs. Though the renovations we've planned will mean a slowdown in business for a few months." He paused to study her. "Can you handle a slowdown?"

Holly gaped at him until the words sank in. She could keep the shop open! She laughed for sheer relief. "You bet. That's fantastic news. Thank you, Brady."

She longed to fling her arms around him. If only he loved her...

"You're very welcome. But that's not all," he said, advancing toward her. "I've decided to move back to town." His eyes bright with warmth, he clasped her hands in his and pulled her to her feet. "There's a certain woman I've fallen in love with. I'm planning to settle down with her—if she'll have me."

"Are you saying what I think you are?" she asked, hardly daring to breathe.

He squeezed her fingers. "I love you, Holly. I want to spend the rest of my life with you and the brothers and sisters we give Alix. Unless you're happy with just one..."

"I'd like to have a few more. I love kids."

"You said I'd make a good father. I'm ready to be Alix's dad. Once she gets used to the idea. Maybe we'll hire Monica to sell us a house with a big yard and lots of bedrooms. What do you think?"

"I think... I love you, too, Brady. I always have."

"Is that a yes?"

"It certainly is."

"Wahoo!" Aileen shouted through the door.

"Eavesdropper," Holly scolded through a grin that refused to dim.

"Time to leave, Aileen," Brady said. "Lock the door behind you and put out the Closed sign, will you?"

After the door clicked, he pulled Holly into his arms. "Now, where were we?"

Filled with joy and love, she wrapped her arms around his neck. "Right where we're supposed to be."

* * * * *

THE ROYAL HOUSE OF NIROLI
Always passionate, always proud

The richest royal family in the world—united by blood
and passion, torn apart by deceit and desire

Nestled in the azure blue of the Mediterranean Sea, the majestic
island of Niroli has prospered for centuries. The Fierezza men
have worn the crown with passion and pride since ancient
times. But now, as the king's health declines, and his two sons
have been tragically killed, the crown is in jeopardy.

The clock is ticking—a new heir must be found before the
king is forced to abdicate. By royal decree the internationally
scattered members of the Fierezza family are summoned to
claim their destiny. But any person who takes the throne must
do so according to The Rules of the Royal House of Niroli.
Soon secrets and rivalries emerge as the descendants of this
ancient royal line vie for position and power. Only a true
Fierezza can become ruler—a person dedicated to their
country, their people…and their eternal love!

Each month starting in July 2007,
Harlequin Presents is delighted to bring you
an exciting installment from
THE ROYAL HOUSE OF NIROLI,
in which you can follow the epic search
for the true Nirolian king.
Eight heirs, eight romances, eight fantastic stories!

Here's your chance to enjoy a sneak preview of the first
book delivered to you by royal decree…

FIVE minutes later she was standing immobile in front of the study's window, her original purpose of coming in forgotten, as she stared in shocked horror at the envelope she was holding. Waves of heat followed by icy chill surged through her body. She could hardly see the address now through her blurred vision, but the crest on its left-hand front corner stood out, its *royal* crest, followed by the address: *HRH Prince Marco of Niroli...*

She didn't hear Marco's key in the apartment door, she didn't even hear him calling out her name. Her shock was so great that nothing could penetrate it. It encased her in a kind of bubble, which only concentrated the torment of what she was suffering and branded it on her brain so that it could never be forgotten. It was only finally pierced by the sudden opening of the study door as Marco walked in.

"Welcome home, *Your Highness.* I suppose I ought to curtsy." She waited, praying that he would laugh and tell her that she had got it all wrong, that the envelope she was holding, addressing him as Prince Marco of Niroli, was some silly mistake. But like a tiny candle flame shivering vulnerably in the dark, her hope trembled fearfully. And then the look in Marco's eyes extinguished it as cruelly as a hand placed callously over a dying person's face to stem their last breath.

"Give that to me," he demanded, taking the envelope from her.

"It's too late, Marco," Emily told him brokenly. "I know the truth now…." She dug her teeth in her lower lip to try to force back her own pain.

"You had no right to go through my desk," Marco shot back at her furiously, full of loathing at being caught off-guard and forced into a position in which he was in the wrong, making him determined to find something he could accuse Emily of. "I trusted you…."

Emily could hardly believe what she was hearing. "No, you didn't trust me, Marco, and you didn't trust me because you knew that I couldn't trust you. And you knew that because you're a liar, and liars don't trust people because they know that they themselves cannot be trusted." She not only felt sick, she also felt as though she could hardly breathe. "You are Prince Marco of Niroli…. How could you not tell me who you are and still live with me as intimately as we have lived together?" she demanded brokenly.

"Stop being so ridiculously dramatic," Marco demanded fiercely. "You are making too much of the situation."

"*Too much?*" Emily almost screamed the words at him. "When were you going to tell me, Marco? Perhaps you just planned to walk away without telling me anything? After all, what do my feelings matter to you?"

"Of course they matter." Marco stopped her sharply. "And it was in part to protect them, and you, that I decided not to inform you when my grandfather first announced that he intended to step down from the throne and hand it on to me."

"To protect me?" Emily nearly choked on her fury. "Hand on the throne? No wonder you told me when you first took me to bed that all you wanted was sex. You *knew* that was the only kind of relationship there could ever be between us! You *knew* that one day you would be Niroli's king. No doubt you are expected to marry a princess. Is she picked out for you already, your *royal* bride?"

* * * * *

Look for THE FUTURE KING'S PREGNANT MISTRESS
by Penny Jordan in July 2007,
from Harlequin Presents,
available wherever books are sold.

® HARLEQUIN®

Mediterranean
N I G H T S™

Experience the glamour and elegance of cruising the
high seas with a new 12-book series....

MEDITERRANEAN NIGHTS

Coming in July 2007...

SCENT OF A WOMAN

by

Joanne Rock

When Danielle Chevalier is invited to an exclusive conference aboard *Alexandra's Dream*, she knows it will mean good things for her struggling fragrance company. But her dreams get a setback when she meets Adam Burns, a representative from a large American conglomerate.

Danielle is charmed by the brusque American—until she finds out he means to compete with her bid for the opportunity that will save her family business!

Do you know
a real-life heroine?

Nominate her for the Harlequin
More Than Words award.

Each year Harlequin Enterprises honors five
ordinary women for their extraordinary
commitment to their community.

Each recipient of the Harlequin More Than Words
award receives a $10,000 donation from Harlequin
to advance the work of her chosen charity. And five
of Harlequin's most acclaimed authors donate their
time and creative talents to writing a novella inspired
by the award recipients. The More Than Words
anthology is published annually in October and all
proceeds benefit causes of concern to women.

HARLEQUIN

More Than Words

**For more details or to nominate
a woman you know please visit**

www.HarlequinMoreThanWords.com

nocturne™

**DON'T MISS THE RIVETING CONCLUSION
TO THE RAINTREE TRILOGY**

RAINTREE: SANCTUARY

by *New York Times* bestselling author

BEVERLY
BARTON

Mercy, guardian of the Raintree
homeplace, takes a stand against
the Ansara wizards to battle for
the Clan's future.

*On sale July,
wherever books are sold.*

THE GARRISONS
A brand-new family saga begins with

THE CEO'S SCANDALOUS AFFAIR
BY ROXANNE ST. CLAIRE

Eldest son Parker Garrison is preoccupied running his Miami hotel empire and dealing with his recently deceased father's secret second family. Since he has little time to date, taking his superefficient assistant to a charity event should have been a simple plan. Until passion takes them beyond business.

Don't miss any of the six exciting titles in **THE GARRISONS** continuity, beginning in July. Only from Silhouette Desire.

THE CEO'S SCANDALOUS AFFAIR
#1807

Available July 2007.

REQUEST YOUR FREE BOOKS!

2 FREE NOVELS PLUS 2
FREE GIFTS!

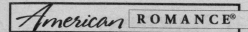

American ROMANCE®

Heart, Home & Happiness!

YES! Please send me 2 FREE Harlequin American Romance® novels and my 2 FREE gifts. After receiving them, if I don't wish to receive any more books, I can return the shipping statement marked "cancel." If I don't cancel, I will receive 4 brand-new novels every month and be billed just $4.24 per book in the U.S., or $4.99 per book in Canada, plus 25¢ shipping and handling per book and applicable taxes, if any*. That's a savings of close to 15% off the cover price! I understand that accepting the 2 free books and gifts places me under no obligation to buy anything. I can always return a shipment and cancel at any time. Even if I never buy another book from Harlequin, the two free books and gifts are mine to keep forever.

154 HDN EEZK   354 HDN EEZV

Name	(PLEASE PRINT)
Address	Apt. #
City	State/Prov. Zip/Postal Code

Signature (if under 18, a parent or guardian must sign)

Mail to the **Harlequin Reader Service®:**
IN U.S.A.: P.O. Box 1867, Buffalo, NY 14240-1867
IN CANADA: P.O. Box 609, Fort Erie, Ontario L2A 5X3

Not valid to current Harlequin American Romance subscribers.

**Want to try two free books from another line?
Call 1-800-873-8635 or visit www.morefreebooks.com.**

* Terms and prices subject to change without notice. NY residents add applicable sales tax. Canadian residents will be charged applicable provincial taxes and GST. This offer is limited to one order per household. All orders subject to approval. Credit or debit balances in a customer's account(s) may be offset by any other outstanding balance owed by or to the customer. Please allow 4 to 6 weeks for delivery.

Your Privacy: Harlequin is committed to protecting your privacy. Our Privacy Policy is available online at www.eHarlequin.com or upon request from the Reader Service. From time to time we make our lists of customers available to reputable firms who may have a product or service of interest to you. If you would prefer we not share your name and address, please check here. ☐

HAR0